dunno

dunno

Peter Inson

Charles Kimpton

First published in 2004

By Charles Kimpton Publishers, 15. Priory Crescent, Sudbury, Middlesex.
HA0 2QQ

Cover design by Dave Newbery, with acknowledgements to
Nick Danziger for the use of material from The British, pub. HarperCollins.
[ISBN 0-00-257159-5]

Editing: Miriam Richardson.

ISBN 0-9547614-0-5

Printed by Antony Rowe of Chippenham, Wilts.

Acknowledgements

To Graham and Margaret, who gave me straight answers to questions, to Miriam, Nick and Dave who patiently encouraged me and to some even younger people who provided important comments and suggestions:

Apoorv,
Daniela,
Duncan,
Jessica,
Marc,
Nadia,
Nat,
Pasha
and Sammy.

Chapter One

The glass broke easily. He dropped the stone and noticed the blood dripping onto the windowsill. Slowly, he turned his arm and watched the red line run down to the elbow and fall away. He saw the first splash on the step and then the pain struck at him, a sharp stinging pain that took a hold more and more. A cold wind cut at him under his T-shirt and he struggled to see what he had done. His other hand felt for the nearer pocket, which was empty, then tried to reach a handkerchief from the other side. "Shit!" There were more splashes, this time on the door, and the mess troubled him.

He had to reach inside the broken window with his injured arm so the blood followed his hand round to the door handle. As soon as he had stepped inside he slammed the door and went through to the kitchen where he found the remains of some paper towel. He seized it with a bloody left hand and tore off a piece. The wound did not look very big, no bigger than some he had had before, but it continued to weep.

He glanced quickly into the top drawers then hurried upstairs to his mother's bedroom. He found what he wanted in the second drawer down, mainly used fivers which he stuffed into his pockets. He lifted his arm again to look at the blood and noticed the photograph above the chest of drawers. The familiar faces stared back at him. He had seen them hundreds of times before; the younger girl was his mother, but he knew little about the others. He ignored them now and quickly left the house.

"What are you doing home so early?" The old woman from round the corner stared at him through thick glasses. He wanted to shove her to one side where she could not poke her nose in. She was worse than the little kids in the next street.

"Mind your own sodding . . . " He walked on, head down. He

could feel the wetness of the blood against his cold skin and wondered where he would find the other boy.

Across the green stood the empty house where he had first met Dean. Jon turned up the path and pushed at the front door. Inside, there was silence. Other people's words shouted back at him from the walls where they had been sprayed, confused, as if the writers had been fighting over a collection of old cans. Some of them still littered the floor. He paused: who was Tracey?

"You there, Dean?" There was no response.

Jon swung out of the house and walked on. At the next corner, halfway to the park, he ran into some of the girls from his class. The tall, thin one, the one whose name he couldn't remember, stepped out in front of him. Immediately, he knew that he would not be able to cope with her; older boys enjoyed her presence but she always terrified him. Whenever he saw her he tried to escape her angular hardness – she had no figure, no curves to fend him off with – but he was drawn closer, closer to the voice which rattled him with its false friendliness. She stood there, insistent, arrogant, a sort of flat-chested page-three girl. Like the girls in the ads, she meant to bother him. Her mates giggled.

"Where yer been since lunch then? Miss Lambert was askin' for yer."

Jon ignored her but she towered over him, her head twisted downwards, almost striking at him like a bird of prey and moving with him as he tried to walk past. He was spiked, skewered, and he asked himself why these bloody girls wouldn't run away like they used to. Instead, she was coming after him, demanding his attention. Why should he turn back?

"Ah, fuck off you old slag." He shifted his path, pushed her to one side and walked on. For the other girls this was a signal to join in and they screeched at him as only girls can. Desperate, head down, Jon hurried away.

Away from their noise and questions he broke into a slow run and didn't stop until he had reached the other side of the park. He was panting heavily now as, in front of him, he could see the top of Dean's head over on the other side of the old car. Without waiting to get his breath he walked round to the other boy. Dean looked at him and grinned. He was leaning against the car like a salesman outside a smart showroom, about to sell him a real bargain. His arms were crossed over his chest and he had swung one leg across the other.

"I got it." Jon held out the notes.

Dean took them and started to count the money. "Hey, what's all this?" The older boy held up a blood-stained note. "This is no bloody use. What the 'ell've you been doing?"

"I cut meself. They'll dry all right." He held his hand out, not to take back the notes, but to indicate to the other boy that they would be all right.

"What d'yer think I am?" The older boy gripped the notes. "I'll need some more – these ain't a lot of use, are they?"

"These'll count for half."

Dean paused and looked at Jon. "You still owe me half, right? Anyway, where did yer get this crap from?"

Jon turned away slightly and kicked at a small piece of waste wood that lay near his feet. The wind still blew cold under his T-shirt and he gripped his arms about his chest.

"Found a house open – the old woman must have gone out for a few minutes, silly cow. I was lucky – found it dead quick."

"What about the arm, then? How d'ya do that?"

"Bit a' wire – getting through a fence. It don't hurt, though."

"Another two hundred then, by Monday. Okay?" There was no reply. "D'yer 'ear me?"

Jon wanted to be off. Dean saw him nod his head.

"And get that arm fixed, Jon – you're a bloody mess."

Jon walked off, then turned suddenly. Dean stared back at him and called out, "You're a useless little bleeder." Jon swung slowly away again and the other boy shouted this time: "Don't forget!"

Jon shivered his way back across the windswept park. He was hungry and he had to find yet more money. Then there was the empty purse to explain next time he saw his mother, and the window. He set off towards the supermarket now, walking faster in the gathering darkness. They would be stacking up the boxes outside and the others would not be there until later.

Getting into the place where the food was sorted for shelving was easy – so many of them were busy humping rubbish outside in bulging plastic sacks. In no time he had entered by the bread counter, grabbed a loaf and disappeared. He did not hesitate to ask himself whether he should do something – he just did it. He was hungry, very hungry. His stomach hurt and, like a desperate animal, he would not rest until he had got rid of the awful gnawing in his guts. There was no thought of what would happen if things went wrong; he needed food and he got it. As he left, he noticed the security man on the door, busy lighting a cigarette. Jon smiled to himself – he might as well have been invisible.

For as long as he could remember, Jon had practised being invisible. He remembered his mother striking the side of his head and shouting once when she had caught him going through her things. That was when he started to become invisible so grown-ups couldn't get to him. Then there was no looking back.

Jon enjoyed his invisibility. He was like a hamster that learns that there are good times and bad times to come out of its cage. When there was something to eat, or something good on television, out he came but the minute he was mishandled, as soon as people turned nasty, he returned to his hole, to his invisibility. He found that no one bothered him when he was in his hole. So Jon kept hiding, kept invisible, stayed in his room.

He thought of his mother's voice, rising up the stairs and penetrating the door. It was the sort of adult voice that knows before it speaks that it will be ignored.

"You coming down, Jon?" He could hear her talking to a visitor. "Jon, I'm calling yer. Tony's here."

There was the sound of youthful feet on the stairs. "Hi Jon. Yer mum says you've ter come out."

The hamster remained silent as well as invisible.

The visitor stepped on to the landing and knocked at the door. "You comin', Jon?" He needed an answer.

"What d'you want?"

The boy stepped inside and stood at the foot of the bed. Jon was watching a small television set.

"Hey, look at that, it's fantastic!"

"Can't. Me mum says I've ter play out."

Tony looked at Jon. "Sod that. Stay and watch this."

"Nah – she'll get on to me dad."

One monster had just seized another by the throat, and blood was spurting out. The victim slowly collapsed as two more creatures reared up behind them. The screen flashed and flickered then the adverts took over. Jon did not move.

"See yer then, Jon." Tony's feet clattered down the stairs, and peace returned.

Downstairs all was quiet. When Jon realised that his mother had also gone out, he went down to the kitchen. He hurried to the fridge and snatched open the door. There was nothing there so he reached into a cupboard, grabbed the last bag of crisps and retreated to his room.

There had been a time when other kids would take him home to fridges that were full, in places that were warm and welcoming. They had toys and games. He remembered his mother's anger once when a parent had come to reclaim a plastic car he had taken a liking to: "Why," she had asked in exasperation, "why did you leave the bloody thing in the front garden? So's everyone could see it?" After that he sensed the other kids' wariness.

Once, he remembered a mother calling out, "Can't you get those kids to play outside?" A sort of uncle turned to Jon and the other little boy: "Go on you little buggers, 'op it."

On another occasion he wondered what another mother had meant: "I don't mind the poor little bleeder coming round 'ere but that woman should never 'ave 'ad 'im. Anyway, 'e stays out a' doors. 'Es not coming in the 'ouse again." Something about her tone reminded him of the police and soldiers he sometimes saw on television, peering into things, giving orders and taking people away.

The gnawing in his guts eased. So long as he didn't rush, his mother would have gone out again by the time he got back home. Even if he got no more to eat he could get his head down for a few hours. He'd think about school in the morning.

He let himself into the house – with his key this time. Inside the hall he glanced at the floor where the glass had fallen. It had gone from there, but a few pieces remained outside where his blood had dripped. It was the old woman's job to clear that up. Anyway, he was content to live in a mess of his own making – his own room was barely habitable, with the bed half-buried beneath unsorted possessions.

He was right – the fridge was empty. He switched on the

television and threw himself onto the sofa. The fabric along the edge had worn thin and now there was a long, jagged tear. He got up to find a cushion to cover the rough edges, then sat down again. He remembered seeing a can of lager somewhere in the kitchen, set off, and returned with two. From his pocket he took out a lighter and lit the gas fire. The television screen flickered in front of him. He found the remote by his feet, lifted it slowly and pointed it forwards. Background music filled the room and he allowed himself to sink back. He opened one of the cans, drank greedily then looked again at the cut on his arm. The bleeding had stopped and a long ribbon of dried blood stretched across the white skin. For an hour or so he sat there.

It was easier like this. From time to time he changed the channel and there would be a moment's flickering and a splutter of sound as the picture returned. Jon scarcely blinked, waiting intently for some excitement. He waited for something to happen, something to excite him, to motivate him, to fight off the constant bloody boredom which engulfed him. Inside, these things gripped him, but he could not think of a way to break out. The skin on his knuckles glowed white as he cursed at the handful of channels that let him down one after another. But they kept the world at bay: the neighbours, the other kids, the cold, his hunger, even his mother. The second can of lager helped, too.

Up on the shelf behind the sofa, there she was watching him, always bloody watching him. For a moment he wanted to smash the photograph and grind it into the floor but he couldn't bring himself even to touch it. He knew that if he did he would not put it down again. His mother got worked up about the past – why, he didn't know, it was one of those things they just didn't talk about. The photograph was of a girl, just like the girls in his class at school.

Jon shook his head and leaned forward, reaching out for one of the cans. Clumsily, he knocked it with the back of his hand and it toppled over, empty. He stretched out for the loaf and found only the remains of the plastic bag. Unsteadily he got to his feet and shoved the sofa back against the shelf. He reached the door and made for the stairs. As he went, the girl's photograph fell face forward. The glass rattled in the frame but did not break. Jon turned, half aware, then trudged on up the stairs.

6

Chapter Two

Two things woke him the next morning: the sound of the radio downstairs and the morning light forcing its way into the room. Then his mother's feet scraping on the stairs, moving closer and closer.

"Did you notice? Those bastards 'a' been in again." For a moment she looked at him; only the side of his face showed above the blanket. "You mind out for that glass when you come in and out."

"You going to call the police?"

"Don't talk daft! I don't want them 'ere – waste a' time anyway. No, I'll bet I know who it was. I'll get them bastards, don't you worry about that."

"You off to work, then?" He turned his head round slightly.

"What d'you think?" Her hand was on the door handle again. From the bottom of the stairs she called back: "Take some money out the drawer for yer dinner."

For a while he dozed and listened to the voices of the women on the estate. He could hear them approaching the corner in twos and threes, drawn from their homes by the noisy works bus which conveyed them to their jobs. The bus came to a halt at the end of the terrace and he could imagine the women being sucked into the machine. Their voices reminded him of the need to go to school but he turned over and lay still again.

Suddenly he sat up and rolled out of bed. Two hundred quid still to pay; there was practically nothing more at home. He had to see some people and there was a chance they'd be in school. In his hurry he caught the scab on his arm. It wasn't bleeding again but it hurt when he touched it. He got dressed carefully and went downstairs where he found some milk and cereal; his mother must have been shopping the night before. He really fancied a smoke but there wasn't enough time so he finished his breakfast, got up from the table and put a jacket on over his T-shirt. He checked the pockets and left the house.

Across the park he noticed the wrecked car where he had met Dean the night before. There was no sign of him now, no kids by the shops or on the street corners – the place was dead. Some of them would be home but you didn't go there – their families would ask questions, the nosy bastards. Best to catch them at school. He walked on and thought about the kids he'd look for, the ones who visited the shops on the way to school and flogged stuff at break. He looked at his watch. Then there were the ones who'd nick stuff from home, cash or stuff he could flog. He was in big trouble with Dean, him and his big brother. He'd have to deal more and put the squeeze on a few kids. The trouble was, some of them had big brothers. For a few moments he wondered how it would go.

The school was an untidy collection of buildings, an old brick cube surrounded by a number of huts and some old sheds that weren't used now, not since the fire. He smiled when he remembered the fire. He went in the back way and paused as he turned into the playground to see who was around. There was no one – school must have started. The rubbish bins remained, shoved unceremoniously into a neglected corner, but the old wooden buildings had gone. All that remained were the scars on the edge of the playground and some charred wooden posts.

For a moment he forgot the younger boys and the money he so badly needed. The sound of flames came back to him, and the cheering of the other kids rang again in his ears. The fire brigade had rushed in and the kids had pelted them with stones and rubbish before the panda car arrived. He remembered the satisfaction when several firemen had put down their hoses to chase them. Over the fence, over on the waste ground where they had retreated, there were no friends cheering now.

He shivered and moved towards the doorway. As he turned a corner in the corridor he bumped into a teacher. Jon assumed the usual posture that said, *why don't you look where you're going, you great stupid twat? You might have hurt me so you'd better not get on to me about being out of class.* The teacher ignored his unvoiced complaint.

"What are you doing out of lessons?"

"Toilet, Sir."

"Have you got a note?"

"No."

"Whose class should you be in now?"

Jon paused very briefly. He was weighing up the teacher. In his first year he had encountered him several times – once he had tried to keep Jon behind after school. The man stood right in front of him, watching Jon closely with small, hard eyes. He wasn't much taller than Jon but he was clearly not going to move.

"Mrs. Ryan's."

"Didn't she give you a note?"

"No."

"Did you ask for one?"

"What? . . . er, no. She just said okay."

"Do you think I'm going to swallow that?"

"Dunno." He was trapped by words, by questions he couldn't keep away from. They just went on and on. Sometimes you could play for time, just say nothing and see what happened, but usually, whether you stayed and listened to this man and his words, or whether you took off, out of the door, out of the gates and across the yard, there would be more questions. A voice called from somewhere along the corridor. "Mr. Grover?"

"I'll see you later, young man."

He was saved, saved by someone else's words, someone else's questions. He could save his answers, his delays and his dodges and his *dunnos* for another day.

He spent break where he could watch the toilets. It was a cold spot to patrol and his shivering got worse. He tried to keep warm by leaning on a radiator that was almost cold and made little difference to the draught that came out of the toilets. He shut his eyes once or twice but the stink would not go away so he had to grit his teeth and put up with it. He leant back on the thin edge of the radiator and gripped it with both hands, rocking himself back and forth like an animal trapped in its cage. He was lost in his own impenetrable world, locked in by his own hand, but he knew about this other world around him and he waited for it to trouble him again.

There were steps around the corner and he stood up, watching and listening warily. A few boys nodded to him as they went past but showed no inclination to speak. He was pleased that nobody bothered him.

A boy of about his age and size came along. He looked at Jon and hesitated. Jon watched him. "Hiya. How yer doing, Jon?"

"All right." He felt his jacket pocket again, then looked around away from the toilets. "Come over here – I've summat to show yer." The boy didn't move. "Come on you wally, you'll like this."

"All right, then."

Round the corner Jon stepped into the doorway of one of the huts. "Come on – I ain't got all day."

The other boy stepped out of the sunshine and followed Jon into the shadow of the wooden slum.

"You don't mind making a few quid, do yer?" He looked at the boy. "And you owe me a favour."

The boy said nothing. Jon vaguely recalled other times when he had had to listen to older boys, trapped away from a door or pushed up into a corner.

"I've bin good to you since that other business. You owe me one." He stepped a little closer to him. The other boy seemed unsure and tried to keep his distance. Jon tried to recall what other, bigger boys had said to him. He moved closer again. "It's dead easy, they're all buying these. Ah can only give you a few to start with, a sample like. Here y'are." The boy hesitated. "Go on, for Christ's sake. Don't be scared of the bloody things."

The boy took hold of the bag that was held out to him.

"There's ten in there. You'll easy get a fiver for them – you know how to ask, okay? Then I'll let you have them for three quid each – that's thirty quid you owe me, right?" There was no reply. "I said, 'Right.' Okay?" The boy nodded. "I'll see yer Thursday."

The other kids drifted into classes at the end of break. When it was quiet Jon returned to the toilets where he waited for five minutes, then left. The changing rooms were towards the far end of the playground. Jon glanced up towards the sports field, then slipped into the first one where rows of clothes were waiting for him – he noticed the smashed lock on the door as he went in, and smiled: someone else had done his work for him. Several kids had not bothered to empty their pockets. Five minutes later he reappeared, then hurried out of school.

At the start of the next lesson he was among the first kids to arrive. He settled himself under the window, halfway back in the room. While he waited he pulled up his sleeve and quickly looked down at his arm. The skin on either side of the scab was deep red now and the whole area was throbbing.

"Didn't see you at registration this morning, Jonathan."

Mrs. Lambert, his form teacher, had arrived to teach them English. She wasn't ugly like most of the women teachers and he wondered why she did this job. Why did she put up with all this crap? She never said a word to them about it, but you could tell, the way she sighed sometimes, the way she asked the same question over and over again. Why put up with that – why not just tell the old man to stick his job? Jon knew instinctively that none of them ever put up with anything like that – they would shout, walk out or just push their way past and worry about it later.

Why did she keep smiling at him? She followed him and the other kids with that same smile, and trapped them with it – they could rarely escape. What was going to keep her nose out of his business this morning?

"Felt sick."

"Did you bring a note?"

"She went out before I left."

"But you know you've to bring a note. Does your mother know that you were late for school?"

"Dunno."

"Then you'd better see me at the end of the lesson."

Jon turned quickly away before the bright eyes and the red mouth held him again.

He was one of the first to move towards the classroom door. Mrs. Lambert was piling up books and papers and her back was turned as he passed her and slipped through the doorway. Along the corridor, the younger boy did not see him approaching from behind until he had been swung to one side under a staircase.

"It's me again." Jon let go of his second victim and the boy stood squarely in front of him. There was no way past. "Now last time I needed a spot of help you were very good to me. And," he paused, "ah've bin good to you since." Again he paused. "By Thursday ah want some dosh. You understand?" He turned the boy round and walked him firmly along the corridor.

"I was bloody good to you – you remember that kid from Class 3?"

The boy said nothing, stubborn little bastard. "You remember, that fat git, thought he was gonna get money off yer?" He paused again. The other boy said nothing, locked as he was in this brotherly grip. "I really need some dosh, understand?" The boy looked at him without moving a muscle. "And I know how good you can be at finding dosh when you want to 'elp yer old mate. That's right, innit?" Jon squeezed his victim again, a short, quick, vicious squeeze that told him he could be squeezed at any time and any place, whenever, in effect, his friend wanted to squeeze him. "That way I can go on being your friend."

"What if I can't find any?"

"Thursday."

The words hung in the air.

At lunchtime Jon was at the school gate and followed on the fringe of the crowd to the chippy. The tall girl who had spoken to him the night before came out carrying three bags of chips which she held together tightly in her hands. He grabbed at one of the bags and wheeled himself round, stuffing a handful of chips into his mouth.

"You greedy bastard!"

"Piss off, you old slag."

"You rotten greedy sod! You wait till I tell my mate – she'll bloody kill you."

"Piss off!" He pushed past her as her friends gathered around, leaving their shouting and shrieking behind him.

Further along, past the shops, there were small groups of kids spread out along the road. Some of them had tucked themselves into doorways. He made his way from group to group, casually and quietly. Here and there he found someone he knew. Nothing changed hands; this was not the place, but they understood, huddled up there. Sometimes they moved out and mixed with the others for a while before returning to their particular groups. Jon had things to do and little time for messing about. One or two of the younger kids drifted around a corner with Jon, then drifted back. By the time he had finished he needed to see Dean again.

Jon had found him earlier in the day, back in the park. "Wot d'ya know!" Dean had said. "It wasn't that hard." He looked at the notes and coins for a moment. "A hundred and fifty to find. D'yer think you'll make it?"

Jon shrugged his shoulders and turned to go.

"You're a talkative little bleeder, ain't yer?"

Still Jon had said nothing and they went their separate ways.

By the end of the afternoon Jon's pockets were full again but Dean was no longer in the park. At home the window was still broken and Jon avoided the glass again as he unlocked the front door. He lay down in his room next to his bed and reached underneath the mattress with his injured arm for the tear, feeling with his other hand for the contents of a bulging pocket.

A key turned in the front door. He grabbed the notes and the bag from his pocket, stretched himself out alongside the bed and shoved his hand back into the underside of the mattress. The scab caught on the fabric and held him there. Footsteps were coming up the stairs. He tugged sharply then stopped – he feared more pain and more bleeding. Frantically now he tried to insert his free hand under the bed and struggled desperately to release it as it too became jammed. As the footsteps reached the top stair he jerked his good arm and tore it painfully free. The other arm remained caught up in the guts of the mattress. He lay among the dust and dirt and tried to roll over into an upright position.

"I know you're there, you thieving git!" His mother's voice arrived then she swept into the room, stopping only to avoid falling over him.

He tried pushing his arm back up into the bed to release it. Then he turned his head towards the enraged woman towering over him. For a moment he prepared himself for the words, but he was trapped and she didn't need to speak. With her right leg she tried to force him up but he was hardly able to move; all his attention was on the bad arm and he concentrated on holding his body rigid so as not to move it. Frustrated and wild with fury she reached down and seized his shoulder. As he pulled against her flailing arms his injured limb tore itself free and the scab dragged away from the soft pink tissue underneath. She stepped past him, seized the edge of the bed and heaved it over onto its side. Then she stood over him again, glaring down at the bag and the notes.

"Old Maggie round the corner said you were out of school yesterday afternoon. It was you what broke in, wasn't it?" For a moment he thought she was going to spit at him. "Anyway, it looks

13

as though I've got the money back now. Bloody good job I came home sharpish, you thieving little sod."

Still he said nothing. He lay next to the bed cradling his arm, vaguely aware of her noise. Eight years before he had broken that same arm and had howled with the pain. His silence now, his failure to respond, disturbed his mother a little. She stooped down to pick up the money and saw he was immobile.

"Now what's the matter?" She bent over to pull him up. Her physical warmth and softness made him remember how he cried that time before. This time he would not react for he would not give himself up to any kind of entrapment, any kind of control. Then he remembered other times when he had let her hug him, and she had been the one to cry. There had been no pain then and he couldn't remember why she had cried.

"Christ – leggo, will yer!" He twisted away from her. "Sod off will yer and leave me alone."

She saw the blood on the floor. "Look at that. I suppose you did that yesterday, breaking the bloody window."

He said nothing while she looked hurriedly at the arm. Despite her anger, she took notice. "God, I suppose I've got to take you down the soddin' hospital now." This time she was really worried.

He paused, still cradling his arm in pain. Another pain throbbed for a moment inside him and he levered himself up into a sitting position.

"Come on, get that bloody jacket on, I ain't got all day." She grabbed at his shoulder, angry that he did not move quickly.

He glared back, spitting his anger: "Christ, that hurt! Can't you look what yer doing!" She continued to pull at him. "Get up, I told you – I don't want your blood all over the place."

At the hospital they had to wait. The bleeding had stopped but the pain was still bad. He got to his feet and paced up and down, away from his mother and the other people who were waiting.

"You're driving me up the bloody wall. Can't you keep still?" He went over to the window and stood there, ignoring his mother.

For a moment she looked across at the boy. It was easier to wait with him over there. Words and memories jostled in her mind. Nothing but bleedin' trouble ever since he'd been born, even worse since he started school. She remembered the girl from next door bringing him back home one day when he was about six or seven, head down and no words of explanation. The teachers were always wanting her to do something, sending bloody notes about this and that. He was always bringing messages home. A few times she had tried to write something but had given up. The times they had wanted her to go up there! "Must've thought I'd nothin' better to do. God knows what I'd've done if I'd 'ad any more." For a moment the ghost of a smile crossed her face. She tried to remember what Phil had said – "You get in the family way and I'm off!" But he'd gone anyway.

It was on a day out with her two older cousins that one of them had taken the photograph in the front room – why she'd kept it she didn't know. In her last year at school she'd gone off to Spain on holiday with them. One of the boys they met in a bar said he'd come and see her when they got back. She was wondering whether he'd get in touch when she realised she was pregnant. A year later she met another of their friends and this one moved in.

One morning she met her father in the street. She was crying and he noticed the marks down the side of her face. "What did 'e 'it yer for this time?"

"'is drink money. We'd no food."

"Where's little Jon?"

"Indoors. Only popped out till that bastard calmed down."

She watched from outside the block of flats while her father went in. It was cold outside and she waited, shivering violently. One of the neighbours came out, spared her a glance and walked on. Then another neighbour, the taxi driver from next door, came and stood in front of her. "What the fuck was all that about last night, then?"

She said nothing.

"Look, you stupid cow, I didn't get a wink last night 'cos a' you two." He jabbed the air with his finger. "Any more and I'll get onto the police, d'you understand?"

She knew that if Chris had been there, the man would have said nothing.

The sound of shouting, then Chris was out on the pavement beside her. She turned away and felt a sharp pain as his hand gripped her hair. She tried to jerk herself away and winced as some of her hair was torn out. His other hand crashed across her face and she nearly collapsed under the blow. A car drove by and continued down the road.

"I'm off!" he shouted into her face. His saliva wetted her nose. He jerked her head again. Where was her father?

"You bloody listening?"

She tried to focus on the wild, blood-shot eyes. She tried to ignore his breath and the large teeth and the twisted tongue, the dark hairs that protruded from his nose.

He shook her then let her fall to the ground. She was aware of his steps retreating and then another car went past.

"You there Dad?" The door of the flat was open.

"That you, Tina?" He was slumped on a sofa. Beside him was the little boy, still and quiet.

"What 'appened?"

"Dunno really." The old man shook his head. "Doesn't like being told, does 'e?"

Somewhere amongst the broken furniture and the smashed glass, she found some plastic bags and a few things to collect together. Her father was able to get himself down the stairs and the girl followed, carrying the boy and the bags.

A nurse came along and took one of the other patients away to a room down the corridor. Jon's mother went over again to the receptionist's desk. The receptionist shook her head and Jon watched his mother returning to her seat. She turned to him: "I really don't know why I bother with a thieving little sod like you! All this time wasted!"

Another time, in the infants, he had played in the back playground and she had come looking for him. He had kept her waiting and he remembered the headmistress's concerned voice and his mother saying those same words then: "All this bloody time wasted." Now she glared over at the receptionist's desk again. "Stupid cow ain't got the faintest how long we'll be here."

"Would you like to come this way?" The nurse had returned. They followed him to a cubicle. Eventually a doctor came and glanced briefly at them both. Poor little kid – his mother looked more like an older sister. He noticed the arm. No one had done a damned thing to help him – looked like he needed a good meal too. Off the estate at the back.

"How did you do this?"

"Out playing."

"Did you fall over?"

"Yeah."

"Playing football?"

The boy paused. "Yeah."

"What did you cut it on?"

"Must've bin some glass."

"When did your mother see it?" Again the boy paused.

His mother interrupted. "Silly little bugger didn't tell me the first night."

The doctor turned his arm over again, more gently this time. "Why didn't you tell your mother, what – two nights ago?"

"I was asleep when she came in."

"Hmmm ... you're getting a nasty infection here as well as a deep gash." The doctor looked closely at the wound again and picked up a pair of tweezers. Slowly he drew out a long shred of glass. The boy gasped with pain but said nothing. "And the next morning?" the doctor continued.

"If you don't go in when they want yer, yer soon lose yer job. Anyway, can't be after him all the time."

"It's as well you're here now – it would never have healed properly with that under the skin." He pointed to the piece of glass lying on the tray. "Looks like a piece of window glass. How did you say you'd hurt yourself?"

"Football."

"Oh yes, so you said."

The doctor gave instructions to the nurse about cleaning and stitching the wound, then prepared a syringe.

"This will help the pain. It's a nasty wound but it will be all right so long as this young man gets the correct treatment. He'll need another injection here in two days' time. I'd like to see you then so you'd better make an appointment for this time on Thursday. Then in a week or so's time we'll take the stitches out. That all right?"

"I s'pose it'll have to be. I'll have to get a bit of time off, you see, so I might be a bit late."

The doctor said nothing and turned again to the boy. "This shouldn't hurt – just keep still a minute." The boy held his breath for a second and it was done. "There, you should feel better in an hour or so." The doctor put down the empty syringe and turned to the nurse. "I'll leave you to it now, nurse. Just see that there's an appointment made when you finish." Jon watched the man warily. "I'll see you on Thursday, Jonathan."

The door closed behind the doctor and the nurse took over. He was not a lot older than Jon but stockier and more controlled in his movements. For a moment he held the injured arm with both hands then disengaged his right hand and picked up a pair of tweezers. "I'll try and do this as carefully as I can. Does this hurt?"

Jon said nothing.

"What did you say your name was?"

"Jon."

Very carefully, the nurse wetted and then lifted off the remains of the scab. There was some bleeding still where the doctor had removed the glass. The boy winced.

"Sorry about that." The scab disappeared into a bin. "I think the worst's over now. Just hold your arm up while I get a towel to dry it."

There was the sound of a match being struck. The nurse paused and looked across to the boy's mother. She was standing by the window.

"I'm afraid you can't smoke in here."

"I'll take meself outside for a minute, then. You gonna be long?"

"You can't smoke anywhere in the hospital, I'm afraid."

"Well, 'ow much longer are yer gonna be?" The boy's mother dragged heavily on the cigarette.

"Several minutes still – you can wait in the waiting room down the corridor if you like."

The door slammed behind her.

"Good. That's better." The boy looked around the room and towards the door. "It's much cleaner now."

"'Ow long will it go on hurting?"

"Probably an hour or two, but it will get better. Never done anything like this before?"

"No."

Stitching the wound did not take long. Soon the nurse was winding a bandage over a dressing. The boy kept still; the bandaging didn't seem to trouble him.

"I'd best come and speak to your mum now – see her about this next appointment." Jon followed him along the corridor. He knew how his mother would react to another visit to the hospital.

Chapter Three

Wednesday was cold, bitter cold. He could tell that by the sound of his mother complaining as she got up. He could tell by the way she slammed the door behind her after she had been out to the bin. He buried himself under the covers and turned over. Then he remembered Dean and his brother, Bill. Dean had not mentioned his brother but Jon remembered him well. He got out of bed.

"You there?" His voice travelled down to the passageway. He shouted again. He could hear the radio. His mother must be there. He leaned over the bannister. "Oi!" There was no reply – stupid cow!

He slammed the door and sat on the edge of the bed. He was already half-dressed; there was no point in taking your clothes off for a few hours if you were going to have to put them on again. The only problem was trainers – they got themselves lost. Where were the bloody things? He found one hiding itself under some magazines in the corner. The other was nowhere to be seen.

He remembered then the large trainers in his mother's room but couldn't remember what they had been doing there. He must have been about eight. His questions made her angry, he did remember that – what did she have to get so mad about? At the time he had wondered why someone had left trainers there. They were very large trainers that impressed him with their size and style. He remembered trying them on, floundering about until he finally tripped over. Now he seemed to know why they had been there, but he still didn't understand why she got so mad about it. He thought for a moment and returned to the present; perhaps his other trainer would be downstairs.

There he found his mother sitting at the kitchen table; in front of her was an old newspaper and a packet of cigarettes. He went to take one.

"You can put them down for a start – don't want no more of your thieving ways. Anyway, they're bad for yer."

The boy looked at her for a moment, wondering when her face would get like old Mrs. Butts'. He reached for the kettle and a filthy mug. Somewhere he found milk and sugar. He slopped the boiling water into the mug, managing to soak the packet of sugar at the same time. He could see nothing to mop up the mess, so he left it. He carried the overfilled mug into the sitting room, leaving the door open, and switched on the television which erupted with a satisfying roar.

"Yer can turn that row off!" His mother turned her attention towards her radio, and the volume rose.

"Anyway, time you were off to school. No way I'm leaving you here."

"No breakfast then?"

"Get it yerself."

After a few moments he returned to the kitchen and managed to find the sliced bread. He reached over the pool of water that had now spread itself across the edge of the worksurface, falling in a cascade onto the floor. He had still not recovered the lost trainer and his socks readily acted as sponges, soaking up the water, chilling his feet and causing him to slip and slide. In the fridge he found some margarine and a knife, coated with black crumbs. He spread the margarine on the tired bread and thought about finding something else to spread, something else to take away the taste. He gave up, stuffed the bread into his mouth and washed it down with the coffee.

The lost trainer was in the bathroom: he found it when he realised that his bowels were troubling him again. Ten minutes later, ready for his day, he pulled on a thin jacket and left the house.

Ahead of him the group of girls came into sight. Smaller children walked past them, but the girls were in no hurry. They leant in all directions so that he was unsure of what they might do. Some of them propped up the front wall of a house while the rest draped themselves round a lamp-post. The tall girl caught his eye. She smiled at him with her thin mouth but her eyes looked straight through him. Other boys took notice of her, responded to her, but this one, Jonathan, did not. He was nothing special and he ignored her – bloody cheek. Why should he? She rounded on him. He was going to take notice of her, she would see to that.

"You're bleedin' early." She watched him keenly while the other girls looked away and grinned at each other.

He said nothing and continued towards them, ready to step into the gutter. The tall girl moved to the other side of the lamp-post. Willowy and thin, her body appeared suddenly in front of him but he could easily get past. It was her awful understanding of him that he could not deal with and he slowed down as if he were suddenly swimming against a current.

"Miss Lambert'll be so pleased to see yer, nice and early."

The other girls were watching him closely now. There were more of them but he could ignore their racket, their meaningless screeching. They jumped up and down, fidgeting and wobbling, children with women's bodies. For a second he thought of his mother, a worn and faded version of the same thing, but it was the thin girl and her words that held him back and he felt the need to get past her.

"I reckon you fancy that Miss Lambert."

The others giggled. Jon dodged back onto the pavement round the other side of the lamp-post. One of the girls pushed her friend into his path. Without a word he shoved them both to one side and hurried on. Ahead of him Dean was waiting.

"Hi Jon – 'ow's things then?"

"Not so good – me soddin' mother come snooping and found yer money. She's took the fuckin' lot." Dean said nothing. "And I've hospital again tomorrer. You'll 'ave to give me more time."

Jon watched the older boy out of the corner of his eye. Early in life he had learnt to watch the way in which excuses were received; that way he got advanced warning about people's reactions. However, he had yet to learn to act as if he believed his own lies. You have to lie sometimes, he had learnt that, but he had not learnt to act the part.

"Always some excuse, ain't there?" Dean kicked a can back into the road, then laughed. "Just as well I'm a bloody good mate a' yours." Jon continued to watch the other boy. "Well, it's me brother, innit? You know what an evil bastard he is." He looked closely at Jon. "'E'll never listen to all this. Then it's out of my hands. 'Ere, 'ave one of these."

Jon took the cigarette and slid it quickly into a pocket.

"Still on that game, are yer? No wonder you're always skint." He dragged heavily on his own cigarette then turned again to Jon. "Tell yer what – I've an idea."

The younger boy remained still and said nothing.

"Might be able to help you." Dean paused. "'Ere, I'm talking to you, you ungrateful little sod."

He looked at Jon and waited.

"I 'eard." Jon still stood to one side, staring back down the road towards the group of girls who were moving away out of sight.

"Well then, bloody listen or we'll both be in the shit." Jon now looked up slowly. "Yer know that old bat round the corner from you – the one what's always shouting about callin' the bleedin' law?"

"Yeh, so what?"

"She's always down the bingo, isn't she? She must win a bit now and again—"

Suddenly, Jon interrupted. "Why don't you do it if it's so fuckin' easy?"

Jon's words caught Dean unawares. "Christ, I'm only trying to help you. You owe me, so why don't you listen?" The older boy struggled with frustration, trying to get Jon to listen. "I told yer, I'm trying to help you. Now you watch yer chance and get in there. That way we'll both be out of bother."

Jon nodded his head but said nothing.

"I hope you've bloody taken this in. If you ain't, don't bother asking me for help again. In fact, if you cock this one up, I'll get to you first, before me brother."

The road to school was nearly empty now. Jon turned into the wind and set off again. The bell for the second lesson rang as he passed the classroom. He tried to move away, then saw the group of girls approaching along the corridor. He turned and was swept with them into the room. Mrs. Lambert followed immediately behind. She put down her books and looked hurriedly at the class.

"Oh, good morning, Jonathan. Didn't see you first thing." She looked across at two girls who continued to chatter noisily, then turned back to Jon. "I'd better catch you at the end of the lesson." She smiled briefly. Some of the girls sniggered. Jon cursed them under his breath. Mrs. Lambert glared at the class but said nothing.

Before the lesson started one of the girls swung a pile of the books onto a desk next to Jon. The girl's proximity and the casual crashing of the pile landing troubled him. Two of the books slipped over the edge and tumbled noisily onto the floor.

Jon scowled; bloody cow, dumping her books down like that. He scooped them up, shoving them inside a desk to the other side of him. Away at the front of the class, the teacher was occupied with stopping the girl shouting and telling her to get out her books. The girl moved a few feet and turned to pick them up again. She paused for a moment then looked up from the empty desk. She glared at Jon. "Who's nicked me books, then?"

Jon continued to study a sheet of paper that he had found on his desk. Mrs. Lambert watched the girl, who ignored her and persisted: "Come on you miserable git, what have you done with those bloody books?"

"Whatd'ya mean?" Jon looked up.

"Jonathan, do you know where Lorna's books are? Have you moved them?"

"What books?"

"Lorna obviously thinks that she left some books next to you. Do you . . ."

"Course 'e knows where they are, thievin' little git."

Mrs. Lambert turned to the tall girl who was now advancing towards Jon. "Get back in your place, Tracey. Leave this to me."

"But they're in that spare desk – you just look Miss, go on, look, I'll show you. 'E must 'ave put 'em there." Before the teacher could speak, Tracey was bearing down on Jon. She stood over him and he shrank from her outrage. He felt like laughing at her but made do with a smirk. He was trapped and squirmed to the side of the seat as she bullied him with her thinness and her woman's voice.

"There y'are, Miss. I told yer 'e 'd moved the bloody things. You know what a . . ."

"Go back to your place, Tracey!"

The girl dropped the books noisily onto her friend's desk. The class looked at Jon whose attention was again fixed on the sheet of paper. He sensed their eyes and looked up. "What yer lookin' at me for?" He looked down again, but felt Mrs. Lambert's attention: she wanted an answer.

"How else could they have got there, Jonathan?"

"Dunno." The girls gasped and muttered amongst themselves as if he had told some terrible lie.

"Quiet please, girls." The other boys said nothing, but watched the pantomime unfold. "Answer me please, Jonathan. How did those books get there?"

"Dunno."

"Is that all you can say?"

"S'pose so!" He desperately wanted to smash his hands down on the desk. "'Ow did she know where to look, stupid cow?"

"Don't you call me a stupid cow, you lying little toe-rag!"

The teacher was now standing between the desks. Jon sat still so she turned and waited for Tracey to sit down. "Right, let's get on now. Kevin will you start, please?"

Twenty minutes later, the bell rang and Mrs. Lambert looked across at Jon again. "Apart from Jonathan, the rest of you can leave."

The girls grinned at him and left. Jon got up and edged his way towards the door.

"No you don't – I need a word with you, young man." Jon froze, ready to move on, but the teacher continued. "You're missing too much school of late and I need to know what's going on. Are you going to tell me?" Mrs. Lambert looked at him and waited. "If you don't tell me, you'll have to tell someone else."

"Oh." For a split second Jon looked at the teacher. "Me mum's bin poorly. 'Ad her to look after 'er in the mornings."

"Has she seen the doctor?"

"Er, no – she's not that bad."

"You sure there's nothing else?" Jon shook his head. The teacher watched him closely for a moment, but he remained silent. There was nothing he could say and nothing he wanted to say. "You realise that we'll have to contact your mum. The school attendance officer will be asking questions – you remember him from last year?"

Jon had to try very hard not to laugh. It was not easy with the young woman looking him straight in the eye. He was aware of the make-up, carefully applied, her neat clean clothing and her stillness as she waited for a response. Slowly, she was drawing an answer from him. In front of him on her table her clean hands lay still and untroubled, as if they too were awaiting his response. He tightened his mouth in an attempt to choke off the reaction but the memory of the man's visit twisted it into a grin.

****

He remembered a short, older man who limped slightly, like someone he'd seen in an old black and white film. The man knocked at their door. Jon had left his mother to open it then followed out into the hall to watch. That was one thing about his mother; she put on a good show with people who poked their noses in. However, this time, before she could open her mouth to shout, the man had whipped out a sheet of paper from somewhere and thrust it into her hands. For a moment she glanced at the paper then shook her head. Jon waited.

"What's this all about, then?"

"It's a school attendance order."

"What's that when it's at home?"

"It's an instruction from the court. Your Jon's not been attending school. If he doesn't start attending regularly now, the court is going to instruct you to send him, to make sure he goes."

"What the 'ell d'yer mean? I send him every day. 'Ere, Jon." She turned away from the man and looked straight at Jon. He saw her eyes narrow with meaning. "I send you every day, don't I, Jon?" Jon nodded then watched her turn quickly round on their visitor. "So there. Dunno what you're onto me for."

"Jon has not been attending school. We've written to warn you, several times." The man retrieved a collection of papers with his left hand.

"First I knew about it."

"Mr. Fisher has also warned Jon a number of times, hasn't he Jon?"

So that was where Jon had last seen this old tosser: in Old Fisher's office. He wondered what was going to happen next; why didn't the old woman just tell him to piss off?

"Anyway, Jon should be in school now, shouldn't you Jon?"

The man looked past Jon's mother, straight at him. For a moment, Jon looked back at this representative of some vague world that appeared on the television screen, that rushed and screeched along the roads on the edge of the estate, the world from which Old Fisher and Mrs. Lambert came every morning to his world and the world of the other kids. The man's car waited outside the gate.

"If Jon doesn't come to school when you send him, I'm afraid it's you that will get into trouble. If he ignores you, then the court will instruct him to come and if he doesn't, then he could be made a ward of court and taken into care." The man let the words sink in.

"You mean, if 'e bunks off school, I get into trouble?"

The man nodded. "That's right. You are responsible for him. What about his father – could . . . ?"

"What about that useless prat – ain't seen 'im for years. Only one thing 'e ever did for Jon."

Jon watched the champions of two worlds; they had little more to say to one another, their supplies of words were exhausted.

"Come on then Jon, time for school. I'll give you a lift."

Jon's mother stepped to one side and nodded to him to leave the house. He got into the back of the car.

And he had been let down; what good was your old woman if she let some old nosy parker take you back to school? She had watched him get into this man's car and let the stupid old fool drive off with him. She had done nothing.

A few minutes later the attendance officer had parked in the playground, round at the back of the school. Before the car had come to a halt, Jon had slid his hand down by his side and squeezed the release button on the safety belt. The door handle turned easily and Jon was out of the car as the handbrake was being clicked tight. The man struggled with the ignition keys then turned to see Jon setting off without him.

"Oi! What are you playing at?" Some of the kids looked up but the man ignored them. They all stared at Jon's back, the only moving thing in the playground.

"Where the hell d'yer think you're going?" The empty words chased the boy. It was no use; the man watched helplessly as his passenger made his way across the rough tarmac.

Some kids were trying the doors of the other cars parked there and, as Jon made his escape towards the gates and turned the corner, he heard the satisfying screech of suffering metal; one of the other kids was probably using a key or a screwdriver. Jon turned at the gates and left them to it.

Now, back in the classroom in front of Mrs. Lambert, Jon's grin broke and the laughter that he had struggled to contain was making itself felt. For a moment he continued his efforts to control it. Then he looked across at the teacher, so composed, so unmoved. The more he felt this happy natural, mischievous energy welling up inside him, the more he wanted to laugh her out of his way.

Under the chair, his right leg was full of pins and needles and his restless hands were desperate for something to do. It was just possible to move his leg into a better position but his hands, scarred and grimy, joined in somehow and what should have been a gentle moving of his backside on the chair, involved his nervous hands and a tall jar of pencils and rulers which emptied itself over the teacher.

He had not meant to do it. He really had not meant to but he was glad that he had. He wished that he had thought of it, that it had been a deliberate, premeditated stunt. For a second or two he watched as her composure broke. She continued to look at him as her unguided hands tried to pick up the pencils which rolled away across the desk. Her face with its fixed half-smile tried to hold him in his place but her resolve broke and he watched as her anger registered itself, distorting her face. His own feelings reasserted themselves at last and his laughter escaped, unmannerly, uncontrolled and brash. The woman stood there in front of his desk as his laughter burst all around her. Then he stood up and moved away. As he reached the door, her composure had already started to return but it was too late and Jon was gone before the red mouth could issue another instruction.

Last year was a long time ago. Words with his teachers, the bloody attendance officer and his bloody mother – it was all the same – but nothing had happened. He remembered that too.

Even further back, he remembered his last year in the juniors. It had been a laugh. All the older kids had left the year before and there had been a load of younger kids up from the infants. He could have called it the year of "help yourself" – whatever you wanted, sweets, crisps, even a bit of money if you were pushed, you could always get off some kid in the playground. That was when your mum stopped coming to collect you from school, at least his mum did. Some of the girls and some of the softer boys were escorted to and fro, but not Jon. It had been handy that, not having to go straight home after school. Sometimes he could hang about with other boys, sometimes with older ones from the high school, boys like Dean and his brother Bill.

That was how he had become the fire hero. He'd been ten at the time and a small group of them had gone up to the high school to wait for their older friends. As it got dark Dean and Bill had emerged with an entourage, their "hangers-on". For a while the older boy and his brother waited outside school, content to be seen with their little mob, but the younger ones were keen to go, keen to join in whatever juvenile wickedness there was to be had. They bobbed and weaved, pretending to push and shove the two older boys, small, dark shapes that darted to and fro. At last, they followed eagerly as Bill and Dean picked their way across to the waste ground opposite the school. They gathered around a telegraph pole away from the road and away from the school. Bill took out a cigarette.

"Give us a drag." It was a tall boy, one of Jon's classmates.

"Yer too young. I'll 'ave one though." Dean helped himself to one of his brother's cigarettes.

"Whatcha mean? You're only bloody eleven." Bill cuffed his brother's head and laughed.

"'Ere you are." Bill gave the younger boy a cigarette. "Share that with your mates."

They passed it around amongst themselves and the stiff breeze blew away the smoke. The same breeze carried with it a chill that would not let them settle, and Bill moved back towards the road, trailing smoke and the juniors in his wake.

"Where you going Bill?" asked one of them.

"Never you bloody mind."

"Whatcha gonna do?"

"Dunno yet." By this time Dean and Jon were following with the rest of the mob.

There were eight of them. They were kids, kids out on the road, kids looking for a thrill. One of them kicked a beer can out of the gutter. For a few minutes it amused them. An old couple who tried to pass in the opposite direction were not amused. "Get outta the way, will yer? Come on, out the way!" The old people held back then resurfaced as the tidal wave swept past. They looked up and down the street then continued on their way. For a few moments they could be heard, still muttering to themselves.

"Miserable sods." One of the smaller boys picked up the can to throw it at Jon.

Dean took hold of the boy's arm and retrieved the can. The others watched while Bill walked on ahead. Dean sprinted back along the pavement until he was close behind the old couple. Then he slowed. Neither the man nor his wife were aware of Dean's presence and they continued to haul themselves and their shopping homewards. Dean rushed the last few yards in a crouch, then leapt into the air and flung the can down into the bag that the old man was carrying. He turned and leapt again, arms and legs spread out in a huge "X". The other boys roared their approval and for a moment their victims became their audience, aware that something had happened. Confused and angry, they scowled and shouted back at the boys, then hobbled on their way.

The school gates were locked. Beyond them lurked the buildings, skeleton-like in the strange light from the street. A few of the windows reflected back the dull orange glow. Through a gap in the fence Bill wheeled in his little army. Beyond the bare, windswept playground, in the dark and gloom at the back of the school, they found the dustbins. Dean eased off one of the lids, picked up a bag of rubbish and threw it at Jon. The bag split as it hit the ground and the younger boys chased the sprawling contents and kicked at them until the wind whirled them on their way.

"Give us a light." Dean held out his hand to his brother.

"Bloody wind!"

It took several attempts to light a scrap of paper. Jon helped him and held aloft a flare that fluttered for a few minutes. He noticed the younger boys watching him.

"Whatyer gonna do now?" Bill was leaning across a large bin.

"Whatd'yer mean?"

"That's a stupid little flame you've got there." He scuffed with a foot at a pile of twigs and other rubbish. "Try lighting this."

Jon looked around; seven faces looked back at him, urged him.

The wind blew out his first two attempts to light the pile. Then the flame caught. It flickered hesitantly, then leapt from twig to twig. The little boys cheered and watched fascinated as the blaze established itself. Bill and Dean stayed back and nudged each other as the flames reached up towards the boarded sides of the old classroom.

Bill spoke. "Wasn't you, was it Dean?"

Their laughter caught Jon's attention. He moved away from the little ones. "Whatd'yer mean?" Behind him the flames licked up the wall.

"We won't grass yer up." They laughed again.

"But I only lit it." He stood there, staring at them, the lighter still in his hand.

Dark shapes outlined by flames grew and climbed the walls. Behind them shadows danced away across the playground. They were happy, happy in the way of children who have done something to amuse themselves without having to trouble the grown-up world. They stood still and watched this power that they had brought to life against a common enemy. For several minutes they said nothing, transfixed by what they had achieved. Then, somewhere in the background, above the murmur of evening traffic down in the town centre, there came another sound. At first it accompanied the sound of the fire and the first windows splintering in the growing heat. Above them, a felt roof caught fire and the flames roared even louder as the new sound drew closer. The tar on the roof burned and melted, shedding droplets of fire which ran down the sides of the building onto the ground. They spluttered down amongst the boys who danced around in the excitement of mock fear.

Only Bill was still. "Shit – it's the pigs!"

The others looked up, resenting the intrusion into their celebration.

"Come on!" Dean wanted to get them moving. "For fuck's sake, hurry up!"

By now the siren had registered with all the boys and they followed Dean out of the back of the school to an alley. Soon they passed the shops and returned to the waste ground where they could admire their handiwork from a safe distance.

"Look at that!"

The kids watched Bill walk casually towards them. "Yeah, I know, school's on fire. Look at them flames!"

Jon felt pleased. "Must 'ave been them old heaters."

The boys who had been with Bill sniggered and he grinned at them. A keen voice spoke up. "I reckon—"

Bill turned. "Don't reckon anything, d'yer 'ear."

The boy fell silent. Down the road a crowd of kids was growing outside the school. Dean moved forward. "Let's 'ave a look." They set off as if they had just come across the fire and Bill followed like an anxious parent.

Inside the playground there were two fire engines. The whole area was bright with the light from a huge fire and the searchlights. A crowd of kids were standing inside the playground to enjoy a better view, and hurl missiles at the firemen.

A panda car arrived, driven by a lone policeman. He parked in a corner of the playground and made his way over to the crowd at the gates. They ignored him and cheered as a piece of the roof fell in. A column of sparks reached towards the dark sky.

"Come on you boys, move yourselves out of here – you'll only get in the way." The policeman had to push his way up close to the kids at front of the crowd to get any of them to move. "Come on, we don't want any of you getting hurt."

Reluctantly a few of them retreated a little. "Bleedin' spoilsport!" The officer glared at them and then turned and hurried over to one of the fire engines.

The first two stones landed in front of the police car. Not many boys noticed. The third one hit the roof. One or two boys heard the dull thud and watched to see what would happen next. The driver's window caved in noisily under the impact of a half brick. It was the sound of cheering that made the policeman turn. As he ran towards his car there was the sound of another siren along the road. The crowd retreated, seeking the safety of the green. From there they would continue to enjoy the fun; from there they could reach the anonymity of the estate.

But there was no fun now at school. Jon hurried out to the playground.

The kid he was looking for was not there. By the time he had toured the main corridor the bell had rung again. There was no point in going to class now so Jon set off towards the park.

There was no sign of Dean. As he paused by the wrecked car the old woman shuffled along the path. Jon watched as she approached then turned onto another path. She was pleased to see him walk away, the scruffy little git. She continued towards the town.

He walked past his house and round the corner. He reached the alley and quickened his pace, stumbling on the uneven ground. The puddles stretched almost the whole width of the path and in his hurry he got his feet wet. He reached over the wooden door set in the back fence and wrestled with the bolt until he could let himself in. From his pocket he took out a screwdriver and with it he wrenched open the back door. As soon as he had tugged the door shut he stood, listening. There were four rooms to search and Jon seemed to know where to look. A vase in a corner cupboard yielded forty pounds and there was another little bundle of notes in the old lady's bedroom.

It was not enough and it was Wednesday. He stuffed the two bundles into his inside coat pocket and jerked the zip upwards. Twice it jammed. Twice he tugged viciously and swore at it. Then it broke.

As he moved his foot caught the leg of the small table which overturned, striking his knee as it fell. He swore and kicked out again at the table then stamped on its splintered remains. He turned and found a chair in his way. That too was smashed to one side. He stormed into the little front room – within seconds the ornaments and knick-knacks, the calendar and the photographs were hurled to the floor. The family group in one of the photographs caught his eye. For a second he stared down at the group of men and women and children then brought his foot down heavily and screwed it forcibly round.

On the way out Jon glanced at the doorframe where his screwdriver had bitten into the wood. Outside in the alley there were footsteps. Jon waited until they had faded, slipped out of the yard door, then set off towards school.

He was in luck. Other kids were moving between classes and he found one boy waiting in the toilet.

"Hi. You got anything for me?"

"What d'yer think?"

"Stop messin' about. Ain't got all day."

"Keep yer bloody . . . " The boy had seen the look on Jon's face. "Here y'are. That's right, innit?"

Jon took the money and said nothing for a moment. "See yer then."

He turned his back and hurried off to class.

Later that afternoon, Jon saw the police car outside the old woman's house. Back home, he went up to his room and groped again under the bed. The little packet was still there. He pulled it out, found the cigarette in his pocket and sat busily occupied for a few moments. He went downstairs to search for a light and stretched back on the settee, slowly forgetting the old woman and the police car. Dean and his brother seemed less important too, somehow.

He was still there when his mother came into the room. "What the 'ell 'ave you bin smokin'?" she demanded.

"Bloody fag! What d'yer think?"

"Don't you lie to me. I know what that shit smells like."

"What d'yer ask me for, then?"

"Don't you bloody talk to me like that. You're still a kid!"

Jon reached for the remote and the television roared back into life. He turned away from his mother.

"And another bloody thing, the law's round at Mrs. Butts'. Hope you 'ad nothing to do with it, whatever it was."

The boy got up. He slammed the door behind him and stormed out of the house.

On his way to the car he found Dean. He had expected him to be at his home but he was waiting in the road, talking to the tall girl and two of her friends. As Jon approached they looked up. Jon watched Dean push against the tall girl's shoulder while the others looked on. A police car drove slowly past and they watched its progress without moving or speaking. And, until the car reached the corner, the policemen watched them.

"Look girls – it's me mate Jonathan. 'Ow yer doin', Jon?" Jon hesitated. "Tracey's bin lookin' for yer."

"Where yer bin, Jon?" Tracey stepped forwards. Her thin smile reached out to him. "'Ad ter lie for yer this morning, Jon. Told Lambert you were sick – nosy old cow." Jon said nothing. "Yer could be a bit grateful, like." She stood and waited. "What d'yer think, Jon?" Still he ignored her.

Dean started again. "Just think what she's done fer yer, Jon. She's a real mate. You owe 'er one."

The other girls laughed. Jon pushed the girl's arm to one side and made his way past.

Dean's expression changed. "Hey – we've business to see to.

33

Where d'yer think you're going?" He followed Jon round the corner. "Ow much yer got?"

"Eighty."

"Yer cunning sod." Dean's smile was a smile of real pleasure. He jabbed lightly at Jon's shoulder but Jon's mind was elsewhere.

"Fer Christ's sake, leave off will yer."

"Don't get so touchy." Dean watched him again. "It's obvious where you've bin, though – everybody knows about the police round at Old Butty's. Those girls were pissing themselves." Dean started to laugh.

Now Jon was angry. "Don't you fucking say anything to anyone, y' hear? I've got enough crap with the old lady without you lot grassin' me up." Dean's mouth remained shut. Jon continued. "I'll get the rest for next week."

"We said Thursday, tomorrow."

"Yeah, but I'm up the hospital again."

"Christ – d'yer live up there, or somethin'? Can't do it all for yer." Dean was ready to walk off. "Anyway, what's wrong now – not dying, are yer?"

"Got an infection."

"Friday then – no later than Friday – you're getting further behind. Bill's 'ome for the weekend too. He'd like to see you."

Jon's mother was sitting in front of the television when he got home. "Back, then. Police ain't caught up with yer, have they?"

"No way." He saw the packet of cigarettes on the table next to her feet. "Give us a fag." He stretched out a hand toward the packet but his mother kicked it away.

"Won't tell yer again – all that tobacco spilt on the floor. What d'yer think I am – simple or something?" She turned the pages of the television magazine. "Anyway we're up that bleedin' hospital 'cause of you tomorrow. Why yer 'ad to get yerself cut like that, Jesus knows."

When their turn came Steve, the nurse, was there.

"How are you?"

"'E's better now. Don't see why I had to come in – you'd think I'd nothin' better to do."

Steve ignored her and turned to Jon. "How are you, mate?"

"Not too bad."

Steve watched the mother search for a cigarette. She took one from a packet and then produced a lighter.

"Excuse me, ma'am." Jon was not used to anyone speaking to his mother like this. He watched Steve deal with her. "I'm sorry – I explained the other day – you must go outside if you're going to smoke." Steve stood there while Jon's mother glared at him. Jon was impressed. He watched the two wills at work and felt Steve's confidence and assurance; he knew that his mother would leave. The woman cursed but left and the doctor came into the room.

"Good morning young man. How are you?"

"Okay."

"Right. Just undo your jacket and let me have a look. Jon struggled with his sleeve and Steve helped him. The doctor took his wrist for a moment and turned the arm gently.

"Does this hurt?" Jon shook his head. The doctor turned his arm the other way. "Hmmm – young Steven made a good job of this. The infection appears to have gone. Does it feel any better now?"

"A bit."

"You'll have to let Steven dress it again then come back in a week's time so that we can remove the stitches. We'd better make an appointment now, before you go." He looked around. "Isn't your mother with you?"

Steve answered. "She's outside, having a smoke."

"That's not very helpful." The doctor turned to the wound again. "Will you take them to the receptionist afterwards and arrange for them to come in next week? Then these stitches can probably come out." Jon thought that the doctor was going to say something else. He paused, however, picked up a few papers and turned towards the door. "Well then, goodbye now."

"Shit! That bloody hurt."

"I thought you told the doctor it was all right. This doesn't sting does it?" Steve waved the wet swab in the air. "This stuff's usually all right."

"Nah – I just didn't want to go on about it with 'im."

Steve looked puzzled. "What d'you mean?"

"Questions, yer know, questions."

"Oh, about how you cut yourself in the first place?" Jon said nothing. "Yeah, I know what you mean. Sometimes you just don't want to say. Sometimes you can't explain somehow." He picked up

35

a fresh swab. "Anyway, can we do a bit more tidyin' up?" He felt Jon's arm tremble; he was not cold. It was as if something inside him was trying to get out and Steve wondered what it might be. The boy was relaxing a bit now. "There's not much to do really."

He lowered Jon's arm so that it rested on the table in front of him. The boy disturbed him. What a state to get himself into, he thought. His mother's so different from mine – how on earth do they manage anything? Can't ask him about it, though. Jon remained strangely still, undisturbed by the pressure of the nurse's hand.

"Which school d'you go to, then?"

"Endyke."

"That's where I went."

Steve moved Jon's arm very gently then pushed carefully at the red skin next to the scar. Jon pulled a face but kept his arm still.

Steve continued. "Changed much?" He looked up quickly, expecting an answer.

"Dunno."

Steve frowned. "Old Manners there still?"

"Which one's he?"

"Tall one with red hair – used to teach me science."

"Oh yeah. I know, the ginger tosser – bleedin' git."

"Yeah. Know what yer mean. He used to go mad when we buggered about in class."

Steve laughed at the thought; from the corner of his eye he noticed the trace of a smile on Jon's face. Steve thought too of the way he had kept the other kids at a distance. When he had been small the other kids had kept their distance because, somehow, the teachers couldn't get a hold on him. When trouble ended with a threat to get his mother to come up to school, he realised that there would be nothing but angry words, a bloody good nagging, then nothing. Then, while they kept on about something, you just kept out of the way and waited. Once it had blown over they soon forgot, so it was easy. Perhaps he had been lucky, his patience came easily to him.

Steve picked up a fresh swab and dabbed again at the wound. "Still, Old Manners, he did teach me science."

"What bloody good's that?"

Steve let go of Jon's arm and frowned. "Well, it got me a good job

– and that's more than some of them got; they're just soddin' about on the street."

He noticed Jon's face again and paused; they were both aware of where the conversation was leading – somebody says something you can't ignore, something about you or your mates. Jon knew that this conversation was changing, that somehow there was more to it than the state of his arm and the stitches. He looked back at Steve, who continued.

"No – I know what you mean though. He caught me best mate cheatin' in a test. I thought he was going to fetch him one he was so mad. Then one of the other lads saw what he was going to do and he grabbed this girl's arse and she screamed her bloody head off."

Jon was impressed by this. "What did 'e do that for?"

"Cause a distraction, stop Old Manners going for his mate. It did 'n' all. He went bloody mental with the whole class."

"What happened then?"

"Well, didn't you ever see him go mad?"

There was a knock and another nurse put her head round the door. "Will you be much longer, Steve? We've three more patients."

"Okay." The head disappeared.

"Sorry about that. Best get this finished now." He cleaned the area around the wound, wiping it carefully. "Let's see. Old Manners threw us all out of the lab and sent us down to the hall. Told us we had to wait there to see the old man, whassisname, Giles innit?"

"Yeah."

There was another knock at the door.

"We'd better go and make that appointment, then I'll see you next week." Steve opened the door and showed Jon the way towards the receptionist's desk. This time Jon was not worried about another appointment – somewhere outside was the bigger threat of Dean and his big brother.

Chapter Four

It was Friday and his arm still hurt. The wound was healing at last but the stitches were pulling at his flesh. He scratched at the wound and it bled a little. Then the door opened.

"Yer still ain't up, are yer? Three bleedin' times ah've called yer. Get up yer lazy little git."

Jon turned over. With his back towards his mother he pulled the bedclothes up over his head.

"Did you 'ere me? Don't think 'ahm leavin' you 'ere like this. You'll be nickin' stuff or causin' trouble." She pulled at the corner of the blanket.

"Keep yer bleedin' hair on."

"Don't want that bloody attendance man round again." She paused then screamed each word at the lump under the blanket. "SO — GET – YOURSELF – UP!" Jon heard the bedroom door slam.

It was Friday. His mother called again and eventually he did leave the house. He set off for school by the long route and as he rounded the last corner he heard Dean's voice.

"Where yer goin', Jon?" Dean was walking up fast behind him. Jon looked over his shoulder, then slowly turned to face the other boy as he caught him up.

"Time for a word before school, ain't yer?"

"'Ave ter be quick; I'm late already."

"First time I've known that worry yer." The boy paused to get his breath. "Pay day. Forgot, 'ad yer?" Dean now stood between Jon and the school gates. "Don't tell me you ain't got it."

"Not all of it."

"Give us what there is, so it's safe."

"It's at home. I'll get it after dinner." He paused for a moment. "Ah'll have it for yer this afternoon." He avoided the other boy, stepped back onto the pavement and hurried into school. He was late.

There was an assembly going on as Jon stepped through the rear doorway of the school. He made his way to the toilets and waited there until he heard the kids surge out of the hall and along the corridor. No one greeted him as he joined in and made his way to class. This suited him. The kids he wanted to see he would have to find at break or dinner time.

"Well then – 'ow's things?" The boy pushed Jon's hand from his shoulder.

"Okay. What the 'ell d'you want?"

"You bleedin' know – you owe me for them pills."

"You must be bleedin' jokin' – nobody wants them things."

"You agreed to pay for them – that's the deal. Anyway, where are they then?"

"At 'ome."

"Liar – you've flogged 'em, you thieving little sod. You get that money back 'ere at dinner – d'yer 'ear?"

The boy did not respond and Jon shook him. "Yer understand?" Jon paused, a hand resting still on the other boy's shoulder. "Don't forget, 'cause I won't."

Jon did not go to the next lesson. There were two more before lunch and he had had enough of explaining things to teachers. Anyway, the stupid bleeders never listened. Out of class there was a chance that he would come across one or two younger boys he wanted to meet.

The first period was very quiet and no one disturbed him. Teachers were easy to avoid, especially if you kept away from the toilets until they had checked them after registration or break. Then the toilets were the safest place in the school, smelly but safe. It was as if the teachers couldn't stand the place, but this is where Bill found him.

The first blow caught Jon completely unawares and left him leaning giddily against the rough brick wall. The second stung him badly and the third floored him completely. "Get up, you little twat!" Jon found himself hoisted by his neck into a sitting position on a bench. "Now listen 'ere!"

His head was seized and jerked upwards so that he could see the speaker's eye and feel it drilling its way to the back of his skull. "I don't like people fucking my brother about – you understand? When yer gonna pay him?"

Bill did not wait for an answer. Before Jon could reply Bill had turned out his pockets, grasping his hair and turning him with one hand, and searching his victim's pockets with the other.

For a moment Jon was released. He tried to gather his thoughts but could only think about the next blow.

"When? Did yer 'ear me? When's this money coming in?"

"Monday."

"That'll cost yer – there'll be fifty quid interest by then."

"Monday then," was all that Jon could say.

"Listen you little shit!" Another blow caught his face but there was nothing more to say.

Mr. Fisher found him ten minutes later. "What on earth are you doing here, young man?" The teacher looked more closely. "My God, what happened to you?" He peered at the blood which was beginning to congeal under Jon's left eye. To one side of the drying blood, a dark swelling was starting to appear.

"Dunno." Jon shook his head and tried to keep his face down in his hands.

"What do you mean, 'Dunno'? You must know what happened. Someone did this. What happened? Was it someone you know?" The teacher scrutinised Jon's face for a moment longer, then tilted his own head to one side.

"Got thumped."

"You must have seen who it was."

Jon's pained face dragged itself round in a weary circle then settled itself back into his hands.

"I asked you, did you see who it was? Is there anyone who might have a reason for doing this?"

"Didn't see."

"How long ago did it happen?"

"'Bout ten minutes."

"So, tell me, what happened?"

Jon sat for a few moments longer, waiting for the question to be repeated.

"So, what happened? Come on, you can tell me – what happened? Who did it?"

"Someone thumped me."

"I think we'd better get the nurse to look at you. We can talk about this later and I'll have to let your parents know. Come on, we'll go to the sick room first."

The school nurse was comforting a smaller boy when they arrived. For a moment she stared at Jon, then patted the smaller boy on the head and he was gone. Jon was shaking with shock and the nurse sat him down.

"What's happened to you?"

"Thumped."

"I see." She looked up at Mr. Fisher then turned to look at Jon's face. The teacher spoke next. "Will your parents be at home or at work?"

"Dunno."

"Where's the best place to try first?"

"Dunno."

Should I try your dad or your mum first?"

"Me mum – probably at work."

"And your dad?"

"'E's not around."

"What do you mean? Is there anywhere I can . . . " The question died away and there was a moment's pause. "We'd best try your mum, I suppose. Her number should be in the office."

For a moment the teacher waited, watching Jon as if he expected some sudden or surprising change. Jon looked up, saw the accusing eyes and lowered his face again.

"Whatever you do, come and have a word as soon as the nurse has seen to you. All right?"

"Okay." Jon's head remained down in his hands.

The teacher turned to the nurse. "Clare, just let me know when you've finished with this boy. I'll be in my office."

The nurse did not ask questions but simply examined Jon's injuries closely and cleaned him up. He tried to think again about finding money and came out of the sick room feeling a little better. The door of Mr. Fisher's office was ajar. Mr. Fisher was on the phone and signalled to him to sit on a chair outside. He was speaking to the nurse.

"So you're sure there's no serious damage done, then." There was a long pause. "That's what I can't understand. Did he say anything at all about what happened or who was responsible?" There was another long pause. "Okay, I'll speak to you about it later." The teacher put the phone down then picked it up again and called another number.

"Good morning. I'm calling from Endyke High School. I need to speak to a Mrs. Quinn ... yes, her son's a pupil here. Yes, it's quite important." He was insistent. "Thank you – yes, I'll wait."

Jon tried to imagine his mother at work but all he could see was the familiar face in the kitchen. The last time she had spoken to Old Fisher she had averted her gaze and turned away, before staring directly at him.

"What, d'yer think ah've sod all else to do but chase 'im up? If 'e's late you punish 'im – it's bugger all to do with me. You tell 'im to get 'ere on time and if 'e don't, you punish 'im." Before Old Fisher could reply she had continued: "They're your rules 'e's breakin', so you punish 'im."

"Mrs. Quinn? Yes. I'm sorry to trouble you at work." Jon heard a drumming noise and looked up to see the teacher's fingers hard at work. "Yes, I know you don't want to be bothered at work but what's happened is unpleasant and very worrying. Apart from anything else I need to know what happened to Jon so that I can try to protect other pupils." Mr. Fisher glared straight down at the desktop. With his free hand he scribbled on a notepad. Jon could hear the tone of his mother's voice on the phone but could not make out what she was saying.

"I have tried to get him to tell me but he won't. I need to know whether it's something to do with things out of school or whether it's to do with something in school. Jon's clearly not going to tell me and I need your help to find out." There was a pause and the drumming began again. "Mrs. Quinn, I need your help in sorting this out, either at home or here in school – but, Mrs. Quinn, I will have to ask you to come in and talk to me about this with Jon. It is definitely something we can't ignore." Jon knew what was coming – he could not have explained it but he knew the turn that the conversation was about to take.

"Mrs. Quinn, there's been a serious assault on one of our pupils and, unless I can get to the bottom of this we'll have to involve the police." Jon could see her face and hear her words now. He remembered his mother rowing with a teacher when he was back in Year 7.

Mr. Fisher was still listening to his mother's voice so Jon got up, turned away from the teacher's office and left the school by the back entrance. He looked carefully up and down the street, then set off for home.

There was no money in any of the usual places. He found some food and ate hungrily for a few minutes, then for an hour he watched television. His thin frame shook with cold and shock and he sat huddled over the empty dish.

Later he forced himself to slip out of the house back towards school. He passed children who were on their way home. As they swept by he looked closely for the two boys who might provide him with money. From a distance he could see Mr. Fisher at the gate. He drew closer but neither of the boys appeared. As soon as the stream of children thinned to a trickle he hurried back home. He was sitting in front of the television, shivering again, when his mother came in.

"Now what the 'ell's bin goin' on, for Christ's sake?"

"Nothin' really." Jon kept his face turned away from his mother.

"What d'yer mean, 'nothing really'?"

"Nothin'."

"Well then, what the bleedin' 'ell's Old Fisher – that's 'is name, ain't it? – what's 'e rung me up for? Something about a fight – in school. What was 'e on about?"

Jon's head was still down in his hands. His mother took out a cigarette and continued, watching the television screen.

"'E only wanted me to go in to see 'im. 'E must be jokin'. What do I want to see him for? I don't know anything about some fight." She looked around for some matches, and lit up. She drew slowly on the cigarette then turned her gaze from the television. "'Ere, you ain't got yourself into any other bother, 'ave yer? Not over money or thievin' again, I 'ope?"

As she spoke she glanced at his pale, smeared face. For a moment she tried to remember what it was that connected them.

Someone called Cathy had looked after him once. Cathy had turned up with him one lunchtime.

"'E's bin drivin' me mad. Poor little bugger's starvin' and I can't keep stuffin' my kids' food down his gob." She tried to remember what had happened to Cathy, but gave up.

Yes, this was Jon, this poor little bugger who was still causing her so much grief.

"You've bin bleedin fightin, that's all, innit?"

"Yeah." He rubbed the back of his hand over one side of his face and concentrated on the television.

Over the weekend he managed to avoid people and for two days he avoided school. The pain of the assault faded but the mark of it remained. In his arm the pain was growing again and on the Tuesday afternoon he sneaked out of the house and made his way towards the hospital. His mother had said no more about the appointment and Jon preferred to go on his own.

He was not sure of the time of the appointment but he found his way into the hospital without having to ask anyone for directions. Outside the treatment room where he had last seen Steve was a cluster of chairs and Jon sat down there as he had with his mother the week before.

Two nurses brought patients from other parts of the hospital. One of them came out again with her patient and looked round at him as they made their way past. The patient, a boy of his age, smiled at the nurse and the warmth of his smile transformed for a moment the anxiety and pain that was written on his face. The boy paused opposite Jon, adjusted his crutches, then swung himself along again.

Jon ignored the way the nurse looked at him rather closely. When the nurse had gone he got up and walked to the corridors that led away from the wider space where he was waiting. He returned to his chair but stood for several minutes, watching those corridors.

For the moment, this part of the hospital was deserted. Jon pushed open the door to the treatment room and walked in. He stood quietly and looked around but could see little apart from a white screen drawn around a bed. There were voices which stopped as he came in.

A nurse stuck her head out from behind the screen. "Who brought you in here?"

"S'posed to see the doctor."

The nurse's gaze remained fixed.

"Wants to take out the stitches. Said to come back."

"Is that Jon?" Steve's voice stopped the next question. He

stepped out from behind the screen. There was warmth in the voice, something unofficial, and a smile on his face. "Not quite ready for you. You'll have to wait outside for a few minutes – we've nearly finished with this patient."

For a moment Steve turned back to the other patient, then he looked again towards Jon. "I'll come and get you as soon as we're ready." He did not wait to see whether Jon went out but returned behind the screen.

Back on the chair Jon paid a moment's attention to some magazines. He flicked through the pages, staring back at the gloss and the smiling mouths. He avoided the eyes.

The door beside him opened and Steve stood there. The bruise on Jon's face caught his attention but he said nothing. "All right, then?" Steve's right arm was held out towards the room. Jon entered and stood just inside. The screen had been pulled back and Jon looked carefully around the room. The other nurse and her patient had already left.

"The doctor'll be here in a minute." Steve moved past Jon towards a table. There were chairs on each side of it and Steve turned one of them around. "Here y'are then. Sit yourself down. Oh – best take your jacket off first – here, put it on this chair." Steve shook the jacket straight. But before he could hang it up, Jon had snatched it back. He looked away as Jon felt the pockets.

"Just check me keys."

"That's okay." A smile hovered around Steve's mouth.

Jon avoided looking at Steve.

"Do you want me to look at your face before the doctor comes?"

"What d'yer say?"

"Your face. What've you done to it?"

Jon waved his injured arm, as if to wave away the question. The stitches cut into the new flesh, tugging sharply. He winced. "Nothing – just tripped over in school."

"Bet that's what you told the teachers. Any of them ask you about it?"

"Old Fisher, the nosy git."

"You didn't tell 'im what really happened, did you?"

"Course not. 'E phoned me mother – wanted 'er to come up the school – no bloody chance."

For a moment the two sat in silence.

"Wouldn't've thought anyone in school would've done you that badly."

"Naah."

"Someone came into school?"

"Yeah."

"Bloody 'ell. No wonder Old Fisher wanted to ask questions. What did you tell 'im?"

"Sod all, really."

"What about your mother – what did she say?"

"Just kept asking questions. Told her fuck all." He noticed a smile cross Steve's face.

"So what was it all about then?"

"Oh, just wanted summat."

"Must've wanted it pretty bad. What was it?"

Jon paused very briefly. "Bit of dosh he says I owe him but some other kids owe me. Told 'im I was waitin' for them, like."

"So he did this, then?"

"Yeah. 'E's like that."

"What did your mum say?"

Jon was puzzled for a moment. "Not much really."

"And your old man . . . ? My old man'd go mental if I turned up like this." Steve nodded towards Jon's face.

The door opened and the doctor came in. "At last – how are we getting on?" He saw Jon's face.

"So you've brought us some extra work, eh?" Jon looked puzzled. "How did you manage to do this then?" He had cupped Jon's chin in his hand.

"At school."

"Oh. When did it happen?"

"Last week."

"Who saw to it?"

"The nurse."

"Has anyone seen to it since?"

Jon shook his head.

"Why not?"

"Bin away."

"What about your mother? Has she looked at it?"

"Yeah."

"Did she do anything to it, clean it or cover it up? Did she put anything on it?"

"Naah." Jon looked hard over at Steve. "She thought it'd be all right."

"So you've not been to school for the nurse to see to it and your mother's done nothing. Is your mum with you?"

"No."

"Did she think the school nurse would see to it?"

"Dunno."

"Does your mother know you've been off school?"

Jon said nothing. The doctor's questions were different, a form of trespass. Their directness demanded the kind of answer Jon was not used to giving, answers that he could not control. You gave an answer but another question would follow. Steve's questions were all right – they left room for you to give an answer that would fix things – you could say what you wanted, really.

"You've not answered my question, young man. It's an important one, isn't it?" Again the doctor waited. He started to examine Jon's face but the question hung there, menacingly and without any prospect of going away.

Steve had brought out a tray with a few simple instruments, some swabs and a number of small bottles. The doctor started to gently examine Jon's left eye. From the tray he picked up a gadget that looked like a cross between a torch and a large magnifying glass. With it he peered into Jon's eye. From time to time Jon blinked and shook his head. Each time he tried to lower his head he found the doctor's left hand firmly underneath his chin. To one side he could see Steve's feet. Then he was forced to keep his head up as he read the letters on a piece of card fixed to the wall.

"Well, then. I'm still waiting for an answer." The doctor had paused in his work and was standing upright. Jon could feel his eyes on the back of his head.

Suddenly Jon was halfway to the door, bumping into Steve who did not try to take hold of him but managed to move into his path; he had seen the frustration welling up in Jon's face.

"Come on Jon. Let's get you sorted out before you go."

These words were different. Jon turned back to the chair and Steve stood closer now. The doctor smiled less certainly and waited until Jon had taken his seat again. "You know, there's no real damage done but whoever did this ought to be in court. You're lucky not to have been seriously hurt."

Jon's head was down again.

"I think the school nurse would be the best person to keep an eye on this. I'll give her a ring and explain. You'll be in school tomorrow, won't you?"

There was a pause. "S'pose so."

The doctor continued with his examination of the large bruise beneath the eye. "Just tidy this up as best you can where the skin is broken will you, nurse, especially this piece here." The doctor gently lifted a piece of loose skin. Next he turned to the arm where a line of bright flesh glowed along the whole length of the scar. He probed the stitch at one end. Jon started suddenly. "Christ, that 'urt."

"Right – it's time these came out." The doctor took care not to touch the stitches again. He felt Jon's arm stiffen and then relax a little. "Now then, before I go, young Jon, I'm really going to have to have a word with someone, you know – your mum or dad or someone at school. It could be a child-care officer." The doctor paused.

He waited again, waited for Jon to catch up again with his side of the conversation. "Look. You're old enough to understand that when I come across nasty injuries like these, I have to report them. You're at risk if someone can do something like this to you. I've got to tell somebody about it."

The doctor was far from being an old man. He was in his early thirties and had a thick head of black hair, well-kept hands and black shoes that shone out from below his white coat. He looked well fed and sleek. He made Jon feel uncomfortable just by being near him. It was his manner, his self-assurance, that made Jon realise that he was in charge around here and that no one, no one on earth could challenge him here on his patch. Even the lines on his face, that really told of stress and worry and lack of sleep, gave him a confidence and an air of authority that it was impossible to ignore. Jon could see this in the way that Steve reacted to him. He found the doctor's gaze upon him again.

"What's to stop it happening again? Can you see Jon, I've got to try and help."

Steve watched as Jon's head sank again into his hands.

"Right." The doctor stood up and moved to the door. "Now, Steven." The doctor was looking over the top of Jon's head. "Those stitches can come out right away. The wound should be okay but I want you to see young Jon here before the weekend so you can see how this face of his is healing up."

The door shut and the room was quiet. Steve sat down where the doctor had been and picked up a tiny blade.

"What's 'e mean – a child-care officer?"

"Oh, that's just the social. You don't want to worry about them. They'd probably see your mother first so you'd have time to disappear quick." Jon looked up. Steve continued. "What about school though? If they find you're bunking off as well they'll get on to school too. Keep still a minute, will you?" Jon found his wrist locked in Steve's hand. "This shouldn't hurt. Just keep still a minute."

As Steve nicked each stitch the relief was immediate. He held the blade firmly and severed the stitches without tugging or jerking. When he had cut them all he dabbed the whole wound with iodine and took up a small pair of tweezers. The brown stain spread itself over the red of the scar and made it look wider. Jon said nothing but watched closely. His arm stiffened as the first stitch was pulled clear.

"If you want to keep away from the social it'd be better if you left school."

"Don't be bleedin' daft – I ain't old enough."

"When's your birthday?"

"March."

"Well then, a year from Easter you'll be old enough."

"A bleedin' year! Talk sense."

"Listen – in my last year half the class was bunking off. I wasn't, but most of 'em were. The point is, the point is that sod-all happened. I think they just bothered about the little kids. The older ones were too smart." Steve laughed to himself. "Let's get this arm done."

The rest of the stitches came out quickly. Steve tidied up his handiwork and bandaged it lightly.

"'Ow can I keep away from school? Don't want nobody bothering me."

"None of my mates got into bother. Two of them got jobs, on the side."

"What d'yer mean, on the side?"

"Well, unofficial. The bosses didn't pay tax and that. Soon as they were old enough one of 'em joined the army. Always turned up for cadets so they knew he was all right. And the other one got a right good job straight away. The thing is, they didn't need school to say they were good blokes."

"What about money? What did they get? I'd have to earn some money."

Steve looked at his watch. "Look – I've got to go soon, I'm late. I'll see my mates next week, though. I'll let you know about the money side of things when you come next time." Jon's mouth opened for a moment then closed again. This time it was Jon who wanted more answers but Steve had almost reached the door. There would be no more answers today.

"We'd better go and make that appointment."

As they went through the doorway, Steve noticed that Jon's head was down and he wondered whether the younger boy would turn up for another appointment, or whether he'd see him in an even worse state some other time.

Chapter Five

On the way home Jon thought about his next hospital appointment, about the woman at the reception desk and the questions she would ask. There was the doctor and all his questions, but then he remembered that it was just Steve that he'd have to see: funny job for a bloke, being a nurse. Then he thought of the wound Steve had seen to. Perhaps Steve could sort out this school business.

He would have to go back to school again, he would have to. Difficult – he had not really been at school for a long time. If he could get a job he could move out perhaps, and get away from his mother and from Dean. Then he remembered the money he owed. He'd got three days. There were the kids at school but that was all – the police had called again at Mrs. Butts' and his mother was on his back the whole time.

He remembered the screwdriver and the way it had opened the old lady's door. There were loads of other doors, but which ones? He knew many of the doors in the streets near his home, enough anyway to know whether they were worth trying. Sometimes they opened easily; sometimes he found doors that he hadn't known about. At the far end of the estate it was far easier to move about without being recognised, but that carried its own risks. For a moment he wondered where Steve's ideas would fit into all this. Steve did not come from his part of town and Jon could not picture him on his own patch, could not see him hanging about on the estate, or nicking down an alleyway.

The warmth of the hospital was wearing off now – a steady breeze found its way round the back of the thin jacket and he wrapped it tighter – the zip had been broken for weeks. With cold came hunger but the longer route home appealed. This way he could avoid Dean for a bit longer as well. Tomorrow he might have the money.

Now there was no money in his pocket – he checked three times. A chippy loomed up ahead, the sign glowing a grimy cheerfulness above the filthy pavement. No use trying there. They always took your cash before starting the order. Then his luck changed. Two younger girls stepped out of the shop onto the pavement, clutching a greasy parcel. Jon increased his pace and drew close. He had no need to push them to one side, or to knock them down. As he barged between the two of them he grabbed the parcel, before the girls had even realised he was there. He dashed around the next corner and heard their words: "You wait . . . bastard!"

He did not run far but he kept his distance from the girls and the possibility of reprisal. Half a mile from the chippy he sat and wolfed down his lunch. Within five minutes the wrappings were spread along the bench and Jon was on his way again.

The second house was worth breaking into – the elderly couple had gone out. Once he had knocked at the front door, the back entry had been no trouble. It was so incredibly easy. He paused in the kitchen. Inside the fridge he found a can of lager which he thrust into his jacket pocket. On the top there was a notepad. Confident, impressed with his own cleverness, he picked up a pencil and began to write, "Thanks for the l . . . " but the spelling of "lager" troubled him so he gave up. School – couldn't even teach him to read and write. What sort of bleedin' school was it if you couldn't even spell?

Later, another pensioner watched from a window as the young burglar scrutinised the back entries, peering here and there like a piece of human vermin. He stopped further along the terrace of small houses. This time he found what he was looking for – half of what Dean wanted, or was it Bill now? This time there was no anger, no tripping over furniture, no desperate rush to get out. He was still relaxed as he set off down the road.

"Oh, bloody 'ell, only half again." Dean had spotted him near the burnt out car. "I keep tellin' yer – it's Bill you've got to deal with now. You know what 'e'll say – more interest!"

Jon turned away for a moment then turned back again. "Thought you said by Friday."

"Yeh, but there's the interest see, and you're already behind. If it was just me it wouldn't matter see, but there's Bill, that's the bloody problem."

Jon scratched at one of the scabs on his face. He thought for one moment about Steve and the appointment on Friday. It seemed a long time away. "Got some kids to see later. I'll be around tomorrow."

"You'd better be." There was something Dean wasn't sure about. He turned and walked away.

Back at school Jon watched a boy pause near the toilets. The boy saw Jon, but not in time to avoid him.

"Hi. 'Ow's it goin'?"

The younger boy hesitated. "Oh, hi."

"Well, got anything for me, then?"

"Yeah, a bit."

"Wotcha mean, a bit?"

"'Ere." The boy held out a few notes. "Can't get any more yet."

Jon didn't hit him, not because he couldn't, but the cold and the memory of his meeting with Bill on this spot was still with him. He huddled himself inside his jacket. "Gi'us it here then." He snatched the notes and stuffed them hastily into his pocket. "Tomorrer then." He glared at his victim and left the school.

At lunchtime the girls were waiting again outside the shops near school. They saw Jon coming and spread themselves out in a semicircle across the pavement. This time he slowed down.

"Watcha." The girl smiled. "Y'all right then?"

"What d'you want?"

"You talking to us today then?"

"Dunno."

"Whatcha mean, dunno?" Jon stood, unsure how to find out what they wanted. They were such a nosy bunch of cows – you couldn't trust them with anything. Tracey moved forward towards him but her friends pulled her back. One of the others took over.

"They were talkin' about yer in school this morning. Old Fisher came in after break and asked Lambert why you weren't in, then he asked the class." She saw him look directly at her. He waited for her to continue. "No – nobody grassed yer, nor nothing, but he knew there was somethin' wrong. Then he asked about you getting beaten up. Didn't hear what she said about that but 'e weren't 'alf taking notice." Jon left the bit of waste paper he had been prodding with his foot while she was speaking. "Wendy's brother saw Dean's brother in school, wassis name, Bill, ain't it?"

"It weren't 'im – I ain't never seen 'im."

The girl looked across at her friends. "Well, yer mate Fisher said 'e'd get the police in to find out who dunnit – said somethin' about protecting all of us, bleedin' twat!" The girl fixed Jon's eye. "If 'e does, they'll want you first."

Jon thought of the other questions they might ask.

"Fisher asked if any of us saw you out of school, what you did with yerself, but we told him sod all!"

"That it?"

The girl grinned, a relaxed smile this time. "Reckon Old Lambert really fancies you. Don't half go on about yer." The girl glanced round at her companions, then she folded over, giggling uncontrollably. "Keeps on and on, askin' where you are. You'll have to come back, she's gettin' desperate!"

The other girls screeched with laughter. Then, as their outburst died away, they formed themselves into a little group again. There was no shouting at them now, no calling out, no running after them and hitting out at them to frighten them and shut their infuriating gobs. For a moment he watched, horribly fascinated, as they sauntered away up the road. It dawned on him that they were part of his mother's tribe, and he walked on. He hurried towards the green and the wrecked car where he found Dean.

"You 'aven't the faintest idea of what's gonna 'appen, 'ave yer? Ow the bleedin' 'ell are you gonna get the rest of this money?"

"Few people to see tomorrer."

"Whadya mean, a few people? 'Ow many people d'yer know?"

"Dunno." Jon tried to count them; it didn't take long.

"'E's gonna kill us. This ain't nothin' like enough to keep 'im 'appy. What am I gonna tell 'im when he counts this?"

"Dunno."

"Ah don't think I've ever come across such a dickhead as you, not bleedin' ever." Jon ignored this and started going through his pockets again. "You ain't even listenin' – stupid little wanker."

Suddenly, both boys were very still. Jon knew that he could not get away: Dean was calculating and watched his victim carefully. Jon simply wanted to get out from under this control, all this pushing and questioning. For a moment he thought of his mother's questions, the girls' taunts and his teachers' questions, then all the things the doctor wanted to know. Dean's insults and cocky intimidation added to his sense of weariness and he switched off – it was easier not to think.

"Yer still not fuckin' listenin'. Can't you even listen to one of yer mates?"

More questions. Jon thought of Steve for a brief moment then looked more directly at the other boy, glaring at him with some intensity; somewhere he was just starting to resent the bullying.

He wondered whether Dean was going to hit him. He knew he would not be able to ward off Dean's blows any more than he had been able to protect himself against Bill. Wearily, and vaguely, he recalled the pain and Steve touching his face to clean up the loose flap of skin.

At last Jon found some words. "Dunno. 'Ave ter see what I can do this afternoon." Now it was Dean who was watchful. "There's one or two other things I'll try." For once less of Jon's desperation showed.

"Tomorrer then?" Dean stood further away now and had visibly relaxed.

Jon caught his glance for a second then seized the moment. "Yeh – see yer."

Over to his left there was that old Mrs. Butt's place and his own home. Beyond, to the right, was the rest of the estate with its back entries and broken fences and narrow alleyways, a place where he had moved around at ease. Now it was a place where he was beginning to feel increasingly trapped and where he would not be welcome for the time being; in his desperation he was pushing his luck. School was easy but there were more and more questions to be answered there. There was no one in the place without a list of things to ask him. Somewhere, over the other side of town, there was his mother at work, a place he'd never been, but no aunts or uncles or cousins. Then there was the hospital, a short bus-ride away. But that was Friday and there were still three days until then.

Later that afternoon, just before school finished, he found himself inside the gates, tucked away near the large wheelie bins. As the bell rang, a smaller boy hurried past, swung to his right and half walked, half ran away from him. Jon followed. He did not call out to the other boy until they had turned two corners and gone through an alley. As soon as Jon caught up the two boys faced one another; the older boy's hand rested on the other's shoulder.

"Hey up, Terry. 'Ow yer doin', mate?"

The boy looked up at him and tried to duck away. He sneered up at Jon. "Yer don't think I still carry cash around, do yer?"

Jon ignored the boy. "'Ow much yer got on yer?"

"Aw, piss off will yer; I'm skint."

Jon remembered Bill and pressed on. The boy struggled until Jon took his right hand out of the boy's pocket, which he was trying to search. With this free hand he struck the boy, hard, across the face, then continued his search. All the boy's pockets were empty.

As he rushed away up the street, the younger boy screamed back at him: "You wait, you thieving bastard, I'll remember you, I'll get you back!" Before he turned, he reached into a back pocket and pulled out two crumpled five-pound notes, waving them at Jon. "Yer didn't find these, did yer, yer clever sod!" Then he was gone.

Jon hurried back to catch some of the later kids. Once or twice he had managed to think about Steve and what he might find out from him. Friday and their next meeting seemed a long way off.

Later that evening Jon left the house again. It was already dark and he walked quickly for the first ten minutes, through streets he knew well. The old car loomed up ahead in the filthy light of the orange street lamps and he skirted it at first until he could see that there was no one near it. Further on he was startled by the sound of a can being kicked along the pavement; two small boys playing down a side street. He sensed that he did not have much further to go past two groups of teenagers, each occupying its own street corner, calling out to the others. They seemed to ignore him. He slowed down a little, anxious not to seem interested, but pleased that he had found the area he was looking for.

Near the second group of kids he turned into a narrower road. It led to the older housing towards the centre of town. Behind him someone threw a large stone which landed with a crash on the road beside him and bounced slowly up, striking the door of a parked car with a dull thud. As he looked back he heard an answering shout. Several figures were weaving about in the road, in and out of the cars lined up on each side. The alleyway was up ahead, but closer to him were the figures who were catching up with him. To his left there was a dark gap between two houses; without a moment's thought he slipped into the gap and there, at the end of the alley, he waited, huddled in silence, and listened.

When he was sure he was no longer being followed, he climbed a fence into a larger garden. His eyes were adjusting to the dark away from the streetlights and he could make out the rear doors and windows of the house. Through the largest of the windows he could see the yellow light that bathed the street at the front of the house. The same light turned the long room into a sort of goldfish bowl. All the other bits and pieces were there, like submerged stones for the fish to swim around, but the fish were gone.

He smashed the glass in the back door with a stone from the garden and waited in silence. The key was on the inside. It turned in the lock and he fell over the doormat. Caution left him; on the shelves of some bedside units, in a large dressing table and in the drawers of an office desk he found what he needed. Only when he had reached the bottom of the stairs did he stop to listen again. Nothing had changed and there was little to show where he had been.

The video recorder under the television caught his eye. Kids at school talked about going to the video shop and would spend hours watching. To one side was a large stack of music tapes, piled up between two large settees. On a low shelf was a large ghetto-blaster. Opposite was another door leading into the office. Here a jar on a shelf and the second drawer of the desk yielded further sums. He turned more quickly now, ready to leave. In front of the ghetto-blaster he paused again; he remembered Dean admiring one belonging to another kid. He had said that it was one of the things he would steal. Outside, the lights of a large car swung onto the driveway and bounced to a halt. Jon froze. He blinked and the lights were switched off. A car door opened. Jon reached up to the shelf, lugged on the flex until the plug flew out from the wall and left hastily though the back door.

Scrambling over the back fence presented few problems, even with his load. An alley led towards some quiet streets and soon Jon was standing by the wrecked car. There was no sign of Dean, so he headed home.

Jon's mother was back at home. Jon left the blaster under the stairs and went into the front room.

"Oh, it's you." The ads on the television gave way to a quiz programme. "D'yer get anything to eat?"

"Yeah." Jon remained by the door. There was nowhere comfortable to sit in the room unless he sat next to his mother, and in any case, he wanted to get up to his room. He turned and took Dean's present upstairs. His mother ignored him, leant forward and lit another cigarette.

"Yer gettin' up this morning?"

Why did she have to do this every morning? Why couldn't she just leave him?

"You idle little sod! D'yer think I want them round again from the education?" Jon did not move. "Are yer gonna lie there all bloody day?"

"Dunno." He was more awake now. He tried to remember how he had covered up the ghetto-blaster; his mother stood just inside the door. "All right, all right – I'll be down in a minute." The last thing he wanted was her presence in the room.

By the time she left for work he was dressed and downstairs. On his own at last, he made coffee and found some stale bread which he toasted.

He left early, too late for school, but early enough to catch Dean. He had just about enough money, but nothing for the interest. That was where the blaster came in.

"I've got the money at home."

"Whatcha leave it there for?" Dean was looking at him closely.

"I've got somethin' else for yer, a bonus like."

Dean continued staring then raised his eyebrows. "It 'ad better be good." He pivoted on his heel and set off slowly, casually, towards Jon's house. They crossed a road then turned into Jon's street.

"Yer mum at work today?"

"Yeah – s'pose so. Woke me up before she went out." Dean shoved the gate to one side and waited by the front door. Jon found his key and they went in.

"I'll just get it." Dean waited in the living room while Jon went upstairs. "Nobody saw me fetch it 'ere. I got it last night."

"What about the money though, this ain't no good."

"Oh, I got that too." Jon took out an untidy bundle of notes from his pocket. Dean snatched them impatiently and sat at the table to count them.

"Twenty quid short. What you tryin' to pull?"

"Whatcha mean?" Dean looked up from the blaster which he was holding in front of himself.

"Yer twenty quid short, then there's the interest an' all." Jon didn't notice him glance again at the blaster. It was getting heavy so he put it down on the table next to the pile of notes. "This must be worth a bit. Anyway, I heard yer say yer fancied one once."

"Don't want to get caught with that bloody thing – it's hot. The law'll be lookin' all over for that."

Jon thought of his mother looking under his bed. He could almost hear her blundering about in his room. "Yeh, but yer could do with it, like."

"How about a cuppa tea?"

Jon went into the kitchen. He could hear Dean trying out the blaster.

"I'll 'ave ter see what Bill says. 'E might not rate this make." Dean picked up his tea and swallowed a mouthful. "Bring it over the green 'bout nine. Dunno what 'e'll say though." He returned the mug to the table. "Least you've got some of this shit at bloody last." Dean patted his pocket. "Just 'ope it'll keep 'im 'appy for a bit. Don't want 'im on my back." He paused at the door and looked back.

"Tonight then, 'bout nine."

Jon settled in front of the television. School had no attraction for him; the younger boys would not be in funds again yet and if he showed his face, all he would get would be more questions. He'd had enough of those. At midday he set off for the chippy – might hear something there.

"Gettin' yer own – what's up with you then?" Tracey stood in front of him on the steps of the shop; for once he had paid for his own chips.

"Piss off." He pushed past her. A few doors along he sat on a wall and watched as the other kids hurried up the road from school. By the time she reappeared there were several small groups on the pavement. One of the other girls from Jon's class came over to him.

"You ain't half in it now!" Jon continued eating and ignored the girl. She stood a couple of yards away, one hand up to her mouth, the other holding a bag of chips. "Old Fisher dragged Lambert out of assembly this morning. Wendy 'eard 'im talkin' about the attendance officer. You'd better watch your bleedin' self now. You know what . . . "

"Hold your row." The girl stared at Jon. He turned and walked off, away from her and from the other school kids.

The sound of the gate grating on the front path reached Jon as he was changing channels on the television. He glanced up towards the window, pushed the switch and ran up the stairs. He reached his room as someone knocked at the door. Jon ignored the knocking while he looked inside the wardrobe, then heaved on the door to force it shut. There was a second knock, then a third, louder, and then a fourth. Only when the gate grated again did he peep around the curtain. There was a man, an official of some sort. Jon thought he recognised him, going away, away from the house. A younger woman followed him away down the street.

Before his mother returned from work Jon went out again. He kept away from the area he had visited the previous night and made his way to the school. There were no kids around now. A car turned out of the gates as he approached them. Mr. Fisher's eye caught his for a second and the car slowed, but when Mr. Fisher got out Jon had already disappeared. Night had settled by the time he returned home.

"Where yer bin?"

"Just out."

His mother reached out and changed channels. "I 'ope you went to school today."

Jon thought of the chippy. "Yeah." He left the room and set off upstairs, returning a few minutes later.

"Where yer goin' now?" Jon stood just inside the front door. He had not found a bag for the blaster.

"Dunno. Shan't be long." Quickly, he shut the door behind him.

"Bloody hell, ain't you got a bag for it?" Dean took hold of the blaster. "Did yer get any more dosh today?" Jon shook his head then looked around. There was no one to see them by the old car.

"You're fuckin useless. Bill'll kill yer when 'e finds out. Nothin' I can do."

Suddenly, weariness washed over Jon. It was almost funny; he just could not find the strength to trouble himself any more. So why bother? Time to go. "Right, I'll see yer then."

"What d'yer mean? What about this money?"

Jon shrugged his shoulders and watched the older boy bristle with aggression. He smiled at the other boy's attempt to manipulate him. "I'll try and sort it out for tomorrow. See you then."

"What d'yer mean? You'd better get this money from some bleedin' where." Dean was no longer quite as convincing; for once, he had to accept the weakness of his position. He looked away from Jon. "See yer then."

This time it was Dean who hurried away. Jon looked around and saw that the area was deserted. He became aware of the cold wind and the drizzle and pulled his jacket tighter round him. Tomorrow was Friday.

Chapter Six

He ignored his mother's efforts to rouse him and continued sleeping. The night before he had been thinking about seeing Steve again and he had slept more soundly than usual.

Outside the sky had cleared so the sun struck him between the eyes, and the thin curtains flapped slowly in a draught. He came to, then remembered the hospital and Steve. Outside the house he looked at his watch and tried to remember the time of the appointment. Something had changed overnight, the more obvious things, the signs of spring. In the neglected gardens new grass had sprung up between broken flagstones and a brave flower had appeared here and there. The very few manicured gardens, gardens tended by people who shouted at you if you disturbed them, remained unchanged by the seasons. It was the wilder, uncultivated gardens and spaces, the uncared for bits, that showed signs of birth, of hope for the summer. Today, Jon was particularly unlikely to notice such things for his route took him towards the old car. There Bill stopped him.

Bill stepped away from Jon who stood still and watched him lean back against the old wreck. The man and the wreck, both dull and dark-coloured, stood out now against the brightness of spring green. Jon knew that something was different but Bill looked horribly familiar.

Bill was twice Jon's size, half a head taller and much thicker built. His black leather jacket was the only stylish thing about him and it stood out above the uniform of jeans and trainers. For a moment Jon looked across at Bill and noticed the change in the face, the narrower, pig-like eyes, the darker complexion and the small, livid scar that ran down the cheek, away from the left eye. The man stared back at Jon for a second then hardened his eyes so the boy had to drag his gaze away. Jon hesitated then looked up again.

"All right? – 'ow's Dean?"

"Whad'ya wanna know for?"

Jon watched for a moment, focussing again on Bill's face which twisted itself into a sneer.

"'E's a bit poorly, won't see much of 'im today." Bill paused – something wasn't right. He too could sense a change. Jon waited for him to continue.

"So, whadya want to see 'im about? Yer might as well tell me."

"Nothin' really – it'll keep."

"I told yer, yer won't see 'im for a bit – yer'd better tell me. Don't want him worrying about things." He watched Jon again, almost wondering what to say next. At length, he continued. "What about this bit of interest?"

Jon looked at his watch. "Gotta go – 'ospital appointment."

Bill stood up away from the car and took two slow steps forward. He started to speak but Jon turned and moved away. As soon as Bill moved again Jon ran some fifty yards to a lamp-post, and paused. For a moment he turned back. "Can't wait. See yer later."

Jon did not wait for a response but set off quickly towards the town. He had calculated accurately his distance – he was already too far away for Bill to catch him.

The hospital was set back off the main road, at the other side of a strip of green. Backwards and forwards in front of it, traffic cut a way towards the car park and modern blocks dwarfed the original, red-brick building. Jon made his way towards the entrance, dodging the traffic and causing a taxi to screech to a halt. "Get yer fuckin' self killed, then!" Jon ignored the greeting and continued on his way.

To one side huge arrows pointed the way to the hospital departments. Jon glanced up at them for a second then turned into a long cold tunnel formed of plastic sheeting. Beyond the blurred transparency he could see piles of rubbish and broken furniture. A tired man poked at one pile with a tired broom. At the end, a large poster asked whether anyone was to blame for his injury and advised him to contact a firm of solicitors.

Steve was not to be seen in the outpatients department but this time Jon simply sat down and looked around. A nurse came up to him. "Have you booked in, love?"

"Nah."

"Just let the receptionist know that you've arrived." She smiled and nodded towards the desk.

He got up and went over.

"Can I help you?" An older woman was looking up at him.

"Er, got a check-up."

"What time's your appointment?"

"Er – dunno. 'Bout 'alf-past nine, I think."

"D'you know who it was you saw last time?"

"Er – Steve."

"He's a nurse – I mean, which doctor?"

"Dunno. Just a doctor."

"Doctor Lowe, it was." Steve was standing behind him. "Thanks, Mary." Jon followed Steve into the room where they had talked the previous week.

"Did yer see yer mates, then?" Suddenly, Jon was all animation.

"'Ang on a minute – let's have a look at your face." Jon found his chin firmly grasped and turned round towards the speaker. Jon went to push the hand away, then changed his mind. Steve continued to look closely at Jon's face. "Right then, seems to be getting better. There's gonna be a scar, though – you'll look bloody hard – girls'll like that!" Jon smiled for a second then tried to turn away. "Anyway, you'll not 'ave to bother coming 'ere again." Steve let go of Jon's chin and Jon sat down.

"What about yer mates, then? What did they tell yer? Did yer see them?"

"Well, er no, not yet." There was a pause. "Look, I'll see them this evening – usually 'ave a drink on a Friday night."

"Yeh. I see." Jon remained slumped in the chair, elbows back on the table now.

"Why don't yer come along and see Barry – Tom's away somewhere with the army, but Barry'll put you right."

"Dunno." Meeting just one stranger did not seem too bad, but pubs were not part of his world and Bill got into the pubs in town. Some of the boys from school used to hang around the pub near his home – all right if you'd got mates with you. Then he thought about a job, about getting away from home and from Bill. Steve was watching him closely. "So I won't 'ave ter come back 'ere again now?"

"No – you're healing up fine. Just be careful how you wash your face till it's right." There was another pause. He'd have to see him away from the hospital."So, meet us in the pub, The Railway it's called – 'bout six. Barry'll put you right. 'E knows every bloody trick there is."

"D'yer reckon 'e 'll get me a job?"

"Don't know about that, but 'e knows his way around. 'E'll put you right."

Jon stood up then turned back from the door. Steve was tidying up and looked over to him.

"You know where The Railway is, don't you? Just past Woollies in the high street. You can't miss it." Steve looked straight at the younger boy. "Just make sure you make it – he's all right, is Barry – a right laugh!" He turned to the door. "You'd best go now – someone'll be chasing me up in minute." Jon was ready to go out into the corridor. "Well, will you come, then?"

"Yeah, ah reckon."

"See you then, 'bout six?"

"Yeah – okay then."

Jon did not hurry back from the town centre. A group of junior school children filed past, annoying him with their neat uniforms, their lively chatter and the way they held hands as they crossed the road. For a moment he thought of his own school. No one there had bothered him about things like that. Poor little sods. All he could remember were questions and more questions. Had anyone told him to hold another kid's hand he would have told them what to do. Then he remembered Endyke School and the questions and uncertainties that faced him there. For a moment he paused; he would deal with them tomorrow. But tomorrow would be Saturday; Monday, the next school day, was a long way off.

There was a street market down the next turning where kids he knew did all right nicking stuff. Jon wandered in and out of the crowd, looking at the goods on display but saw nothing that he could get rid of, not if it was stolen. He felt safe among the adults – there were elderly couples who you could just barge past, and mothers with small children who ignored him. He soon lost interest in the market but was in no hurry to get on. At the end of the street he found himself looking across the road at The Railway pub where he would find Steve that evening. He sat down on a low wall and watched the early customers arriving.

He wondered what Steve's friends would be like. Get him a job, get the school and the old woman off his back – that'd be great. The sun's warmth reached him through the open front of his jacket. He relaxed and sat back with an arm stretched out to one side.

Two young men sat down across the way. A tall, thin girl who reminded him of Tracey sat between them. She leaned across to one of her companions and helped herself to a cigarette from the outside pocket of his jacket. Jon watched the man pull her down onto his lap. The girl wriggled but did not really try to get free. The man reached round her and lit her cigarette. To one side a group of four middle-aged men had also been watching. They burst out laughing and, from his safe distance, Jon looked on and shared their amusement.

He felt hungry. Drawn by the smell of fried onions he got up and walked back into the market. A few moments later he was sitting in the sun again. For once he ate and drank slowly, watching again the people outside the pub. Another couple sat down with drinks. The woman lit a cigarette and waved the match in the air to one side of her head, just like his mother did. He watched the man put an arm around her; he tried to remember a man touching his mother. The woman blew a mouthful of smoke at the man and Jon realised that he too fancied a cigarette. There were none in his pockets and the only place nearby where he could get some was at the pub. For the moment, though, he stayed where he was.

He had forgotten to look for cigarettes before leaving that morning – he could usually find an opened packet of his mother's somewhere, once she had gone out. Sometimes she'd swear at him and carry on but he would just walk out. Somewhere inside his head he could see her again, smoking, always bloody smoking with the bloody fag hanging out of her mouth, like the girl over the road with her face close to the man, laughing at him, pulling away his hands.

Then Jon remembered – he had once seen his mother with a man. He could see her pushing a packet of crisps towards him, then turning back to the man. Who was he? Jon could remember him at a pub, playing about, but he could not remember the man ever speaking to him. He only spoke to her; somehow his words never reached Jon. He remembered being taken home and his mother taking him back indoors. The man waited outside in the car. Jon had sat in his room watching an old black and white television. Outside, doors were opened and shut. It was some time before he heard the car leave, and he could not remember the man's name.

Sometimes he asked his mother about his father. On one occasion there had been talk about families and parents at school. His mother's reaction was always the same: "Don't ask me about that bastard – you don't want to know a thing about him." On another occasion he had passed a mate from primary school. He was waiting on the pavement while a man loaded a box and football into the back of a car. He knew it was the boy's father for the man had swept the boy up and thrown him into the air. He could remember the boy screaming as he was caught and stuffed into the car, and he could remember the grin on his face. As Jon had gone past, his friend had looked at him through the car window and waved enthusiastically.

A mother from the market walked past with an older child, a boy of about ten, who dawdled just as he remembered doing on rare outings with his mother. The awful boredom of shopping came back to him and he relived angry moments with his mother. The young boy glared at Jon and slouched on by, sliding himself along a shop window.

Lunchtime came and the seats in the sun outside the pub were filled. Latecomers disappeared into the gloom beyond the dark open doorway. The dark windows reflected back to him the other sides of the people opposite. It was as if he could see round them, could fix them for a moment, without them realising that he was in control.

It was Dean he noticed first, standing in the doorway, waving to someone to join him. For a moment he wondered how Dean was going to kid the barman that he was over eighteen, then he recognised Bill. In their hurry to find seats they had not looked over the road and for a moment Jon sat there unnoticed, wondering whether the two brothers often visited the pub. Then he moved away.

That evening Jon didn't wait until six. He found a corner at the end of the market from where he watched but there was no sign of Bill, or Dean. When Steve appeared, just after six, he went inside the pub before Jon could get across the street. Jon walked over to the shop next door to the pub then turned towards the dark doorway. Through the smoked glass he saw Steve settling himself at the bar, and he stepped into the doorway.

There he hesitated while several people squeezed past. Three girls arrived and tried to push the inner door instead of pulling it. One of them lugged hard and the door suddenly gave way and swung towards the four of them, trapping them like passengers in a lift. One of the girls collapsed against him, driving him up against the wall. He had only the girl to hold on to so they slid down onto the floor. For a moment he felt as though he was drowning under her soft weight and her perfume. He lay more or less still while she struggled to get up, surprised as her legs mixed themselves up with his. Then her companions laughed and he recoiled even further. The girls spilled themselves noisily into the bar and he picked himself up.

Although it was early, the bar was quite full so it was difficult to look around. As Jon stared again through the door, Steve caught sight of him and hurried over. He hadn't seen the girls.

"Hi. Come'n'ave a drink." Jon moved into the bar. The girls had turned into another bar and were nowhere to be seen. Jon felt as if all the eyes were on him and stood in the middle of the bar.

"Ain't you bin in a pub before?" Jon shook his head. "I s'pose you are a bit on the young side." Steve waved at the one empty space. "Don't worry – go and sit over there while I get you a drink. What'll you have?"

"Coke."

"You sure?"

Jon was puzzled again. He went to speak but Steve frowned. "You have what you like. Coke then." Jon sat by himself and watched.

Steve approached the bar where people were standing three or four deep. Jon realised that there would be a bit of a wait, and watched the door. What would this Barry look like? Several young men came in and girls entered in twos or threes, but never, he noticed, singly. He was the only person sitting alone. A voice like Bill's called out from round the corner. It hung in the air and Jon fixed his eyes on a gap between tables where the speaker might appear. For a moment he had a desperate urge to see just who it was but he stayed put; he had to keep a place for Steve.

"Anybody sittin' 'ere?" A man was staring hard at the space next to Jon.

"Er – yeah, me mate, over there." Jon nodded towards the bar.

The man stared at the empty space next to Jon and turned to his friends. "Didn't know they let kids in 'ere – they'll be opening a bleedin' creche next." His companions laughed but ignored Jon. The man did not wait to see whether Jon would move, but settled further round.

Steve came over from the bar with their drinks and sat down next to Jon. He raised his glass. "Cheers mate. Barry shouldn't be long." He nodded towards Jon's drink. "That all right?" Jon nodded. He was thirsty and had soon half emptied the glass. "What d'ya normally drink?"

"Dunno. Don't usually get in pubs. Lager sometimes."

"How's school then? Kept out of trouble?"

Jon saw his grin and realised that the question was not a serious one. "Ain't been there. Too much bloody aggro."

"One way of doing it, I suppose. Trouble is, they can cause bother if you stay away too long."

"Sod them. All I need is a job." Jon squared his shoulders and looked directly at Steve. "Where's this mate of yours?"

"Coming straight from work. Should be here any time. Anyway, I told 'im what's bothering you."

"What did 'e say, like?"

"Main thing's getting a job. Once you get something fixed up things get much better. And 'e oughta know – 'e's 'ad a few jobs."

Steve laughed then looked at the next group. They were spreading out along the settle. He shifted his coat to one side and made a space between himself and Jon. Jon looked at the space. Why didn't this soddin' mate turn up?

"Cheer up. Don't yer like pubs?"

Jon looked at the crowd by the bar and the group hiding the doorway. He wouldn't notice anybody coming in until it was too late and then they could see him.

Steve continued. "They're good places to meet up – never know who you'll see." Jon thought of Bill and it showed. His expression remained frozen and his attention was away from Steve. "Sorry you don't like this place. Couldn't wait to get into pubs when I was your age. My dad never worried – so long as I kept quiet and out of sight for a bit." He sat back and said nothing for a minute. "I suppose he taught me not to bother with stupid things and get on with things that matter. 'E's a good bloke is my dad. What's your old man like?"

"Dunno."

"Never met 'im?"

"Nope!"

"Don't you know anything about him?"

"Not a fuckin' thing – don't give a toss either." He looked away from Steve, finished the Coke and put down the glass.

"Same again? I'm getting another pint." Jon was undecided. "Try some of this; it's good stuff." Jon was looking towards the bar. "Don't you worry about 'im – 'e's not bothered about you. Pint, is it?"

Jon looked back towards Steve and nodded. "'Ave they got any crisps?"

"Yeah. What flavour d'you want?"

"Cheese and onion."

Jon was impressed by the way Steve made his way through the crowd. He was not much bigger than Jon but he got round people who moved out of his way without complaint. Jon felt warmer now and started to relax. The urge to watch the door had left him.

In no time Steve put a pint down in front of him. It tasted good.

"So, you know nothing about your old man?"

"Not a bloody thing." Jon continued staring at the bar. "When's this mate of yours gonna appear?"

"Any time now, I should think." For a moment they said nothing. Steve watched Jon take a long pull at his drink. "Doesn't yer mum ever say anything about him? Doesn't she ever tell you how they met, what he was like, why they split?"

"No. The way she goes on yer can't blame him for buggering off."

"No brothers or sisters, then?"

"No. Just the old woman." He looked at the people on the next table and realised they were oblivious to him. "When I'm at 'ome she's on me back and when I'm at school the bloody teachers are on me back – can't get away." Suddenly he was tense and his glass was shaking. Steve watched the beer slopping about, threatening to splash itself all over the table. "She sends me off to bloody school and when I get there all I get is fuckin' crap." He moved his glass away from Steve's steady hand and thumped it down on the table. Some of the people nearby looked across at them.

"A job, that's just what you want, just like Barry. I tell yer, 'e's the most organised bloke I know, really cool – he really got it together when he was your age." Steve had to keep going, to look after this ticking bomb until Barry arrived. "His old woman thought he was off to school every morning. She used to tell my mum what a good lad 'e was, going off after breakfast without any trouble – more than I used to do at that age. Kept his ordinary clothes at work – changed into them before he started for the day."

"What 'appened about school then? What about the attendance and the social?"

"Didn't hear a thing from the social."

"What about the attendance man? The old woman's always going on about him."

"Oh, the attendance, that was different. Barry's mother went ballistic at first."

"What did 'e do then?"

"Well he 'ad to tell 'er about the job. Poor old girl didn't know what to do about it." He paused and drank again. Jon too took a mouthful from his glass and swallowed, more slowly this time.

"Anyway, he went into school. Didn't give a toss. Didn't say anything about the job – didn't want to cause his boss any trouble. He told the teachers how he'd been unhappy at school, was worried about his work and was frightened of the other teachers – load of old bollocks, that was."

"What did 'e do something stupid like that for?"

"No, it wasn't stupid – that was the whole point. They believed him – said they were gonna help him. All he had to do was promise to try to get into school the next day and that was it. Then he buggers off, back to work. Course it was days before they sussed what he'd done. Next time he took a couple of days off work and went to school – just to keep them happy. Then he went back to work. Simple as that."

Jon was looking up, away from Steve. A taller, thicker-set young man was looking at Jon. Steve twisted around in his seat. "Where've you bin then, Barry? My mate here's bin waiting to meet you."

"Oh, you're the lad who don't like school too much." Barry looked at Steve. "Doesn't want to bother with that place, does 'e, Steve?"

Chapter Seven

"Get you a drink, Steve?"

"'Nother pint, mate."

"What about, er …"

"He's Jon. Can you manage another one, Jon?" Jon was struggling with his pint – it tasted nice but it was making him feel bloated and a little sick. He shook his head. He was not concerned to impress the others. They sat and waited until Barry returned from the bar.

"So this mate a' yours, 'e can't get on with school."

Jon watched Barry closely; it was as though he was talking about someone else. But his attention remained with Jon. Steve spoke up. "I said he ought to be able to get a job – it'd keep him outta trouble and he could get a life."

The newcomer continued to look at Jon. "What d'yer reckon, Jon? If you could get a job, could you manage then?"

Jon looked away and thought of the smaller boys at school and meeting Bill in the school corridor. He remembered Mr. Fisher and his mother's sharp questions. "No bother. Just get me a job." He felt Steve watching him.

"Thing is mate, what sort of job can you do?" Jon looked up. "You can't drive, can you?" Jon shook his head and wondered why this bloke asked such a stupid question. "And no firm can give you a job, not like, I dunno, like W H Smith's. They have to keep records of everyone."

This sounded like school – can't do this, can't do that. Barry continued, "And if they're caught employing kids illegally they can get into bother and that's something they can do without."

Jon listened. They're all like this, questions, bloody questions then you can't do this and you gotta do that. "So what am I gonna do, then?" Now he wanted some answers.

"You've got to find the right kind of … "

"But what kind?" Steve frowned and looked directly at Jon as if he were watching an unpredictable animal. Barry sat back. He picked up his glass and looked over the rim at Jon and swallowed several mouthfuls of beer.

"You want a small set-up, someone on his own or a small business, somewhere quiet, like."

"Yeah, but where? Who can I go and see?"

"Can't you see, mate, that's what you've got to find out for yourself. I 'aven't got a job for you and I can't just send you to someone else who'll give you one."

Jon was no longer sitting upright, paying close attention. Barry tried hard with his words – he could sense Jon's resistance – but Jon leaned forward on the table, just as he did at school, his head lowered. He wasn't going to listen to this crap. Steve watched, biting his lower lip. Silly little fool – couldn't he listen just for a few minutes?

Barry continued. "You can't work in retail 'cos too many people would see you."

"That's a fuckin' lot of help." Jon was almost on his feet.

"Hang about." Steve stretched out and touched Jon's arm, the one that was now healing fast. "Give 'im a chance. Just listen to what he's got to say." Jon remained tense while Barry took his cue.

"Look, you can probably get a job all right, but there ain't no point in thinking you can do whatever you fancy. Don't you get that? You've gotta think about that."

"Right then, what the 'ell can I do?"

"Have you ever 'ad a job?"

"Talk fuckin' sense!" More bloody questions again. He snatched his arm away from Steve's touch.

"What I mean is, what sort of job d'yer think you could do?" Barry was looking straight at him, wondering why his mate had brought along this stroppy kid.

"Look – can you get me a soddin' job, or not?"

"No. You have to get yourself a job. That's the first thing to learn. You have to get a job for yourself. I can help you get a job, but you've gotta get the job and it ain't no use thinkin' that you can get one just like that."

Steve smiled to himself – Barry was starting to sound just like his own father.

Jon was now on his feet; he'd had enough. A voice reached him through the crowd and he stopped, standing over the other two – it sounded just like Bill. He looked around quickly but couldn't see him or Dean. Slowly, he sat down again between the two young men.

"What's up, Jon?"

"Nothin'."

"You sure?" He obviously wasn't, but he seemed to be listening again. Barry continued. "What you want is a little business, not too many people, no book-keeping and no paperwork. Then they can pay you cash, see. Officially, you don't exist so no one can interfere." The kid was paying attention again. "D'yer know the railway arches, down the road from here?"

"Where d'yer mean?"

"Past the shopping arcades, just before you get to the bus place."

"Yeah." Jon paused. "Think so."

"Seen the little garage down there, car repairs, spraying, that sort of thing?"

"Yeh."

"Well, that's the sort of place where I got started. Outta sight, outta mind. But you've gotta be the one to do it." He pointed a finger at Jon, who winced. "Go down there and talk to the bloke in the end place – does cars up – 'e's all right. Tell 'im you've seen me and I sent yer along."

Jon hesitated for a moment. "What about school? The old woman's always on about the attendance man."

"Oh, just give him any old crap – just let him think you're gonna be a good boy in future an 'e'll do sod-all."

"She said summat about court, fines an' all that."

"Bollocks! I don't know anyone whose 'ad ter go to court." He looked at Steve. "Do you know anyone who got into bother over bunking school?" Steve shook his head and Barry continued, "Anyway, they can't fine you, only yer mum. Don't you trouble yourself about them, mate."

For the moment Steve had given up thinking about Jon's father. One minute he asked himself why he was trying to help this stupid kid, the next he was feeling sorry for him. He remembered his own first holiday job, with a local builder, his dad's mate. They'd gone down to the yard and the bloke had asked him to make a cup of tea while he'd talked to his dad. The bloke wasn't daft; it had been a fair test – he'd had to get straight on with a simple task without any fuss or bother. It turned out all right; he'd always been able to get down there and earn a few quid when he needed to. And Old Harry'd been all right – taught him a few tricks and they'd had some laughs. It was funny, that: they try so hard to teach you so much at school and you resist a lot of it because you know what they're up to. Then you meet someone like Old Harry and he teaches you without even thinking about it, and it's bloody good fun. He wanted to tell Jon about this, but he knew that it would be impossible; Jon could only find out that kind of thing for himself.

Jon was getting uneasy again. Steve and this other bloke, Barry, they were just going to carry on at him. He felt stuck and looked up, past his interrogators, then slumped back on his seat. He wondered why he had never been able to make himself as comfortable at school. There, getting comfortable in his place had been the only important thing. Then there was the old woman, bleedin' teachers and nosy cows like Old Butts, always going on. His fury welled up, starting to choke him, but he had nowhere to go.

"What d'yer want, Barry mate?" It was Steve's turn to get them in.

"Same again."

"What about you, Jon? You ready for another one?" Steve was not sure whether there would be an answer: Jon was slumped forwards again on the table. "D'you fancy an ordinary drink, Coke or summat like that?" Still there was no reply. "Here, can you hear me?" Steve nudged Jon's arm. The arm was snatched away and slammed down on the table.

"It's all right, Steve. I'll get these in." Barry moved off across to the bar. His annoyance showed in his face and he glared back at Jon.

"God, Jon. What's up, mate? You trying to wind old Barry up? You want to listen to him – he's done it mate, been there and got the T-shirt. Do you really want a job? Do you really want to get yourself sorted?"

Jon's head slowly dragged itself into an upright position. "Dunno!"

"What do you think you could do that someone would pay you

for?" Again the arm was slammed down onto the table. Around them was a wall of backs. Somewhere over near the bar Barry was turning round towards them.

"Fuck this!" Jon was on his feet and moving away from the table. Once he sensed that he had escaped from Steve he turned and in a blind panic rushed towards the door, desperately forcing his way past Barry. At the door he paused again and looked back at the crowd, almost hoping to see Bill there.

Outside, the warmth of the pub soon left him and he zipped up his jacket. His route took him towards the centre of town where he managed to control the urge to rush straight home – Bill had a nasty trick of bumping into people who were in a hurry. He watched further ahead for traps set by alleyways and side roads. By the time he reached the school and the green he slowed again, confident that he had avoided Bill but unsure what he would find at home.

Finally, he let himself into the empty house. From the fridge he took the remains of a pork pie and a can of his mother's favourite lager. For an hour he watched television, fidgeting from channel to channel. The coming week troubled him, occasionally at first, and then as he thought more about some of the people he would meet, the more worried he became – questions, bloody questions. The old woman, that old cow Butts, the police if he was unlucky, teachers, always teachers poking their soddin' noses in, and then Bill. Bill was sure to catch up with him.

A job, a bloody job, with money and no school and no bother. He remembered the directions to the garage under the railway arches. For a little while the television held his attention. Then he went up to bed. He had almost dropped off when he heard the front door and his mother's steps on the stairs. She paused outside his room and called out. "You there, Jon?"

"Yeah."

He heard her go straight to her room.

The next day was Saturday, an easier start. There was no need for a call from his mother – she was still in bed when Jon left the house. He could hear the light buzz of her snoring. He cleared quickly out of his own area and soon he was walking towards the railway arches which loomed up alongside the road. He passed a few lock-up businesses on both sides of the road and came to a café. Across the way was the last arch. Tucked underneath it was a motor workshop. It was closed. Jon rattled the padlock then swung his foot against the door.

What the fuckin' 'ell was the point? Nothin' was ever going right. How could he get a sodding job like this?

Perhaps Jon was lucky. He crossed over from the arches and came face to face with an old man who was sweeping outside the café.

"What's up? You lookin' for someone?"

"Ah, piss off!"

"You always this friendly?" The old man continued sweeping, getting closer now – soon he would be brushing Jon's trainers. "Come on mate, you'll make me cry if you stop there like that."

He paused as he reached Jon. "Can I help yer? Lookin' for someone?"

"Doesn't 'e open on Saturdays?" The boy half nodded towards the garage at the end.

"Lookin' fer Paul?"

"Dunno 'is name. Bloke who runs the garage."

"Oh, 'e does come in sometimes of a Saturday. Never tell with 'im, though." He watched Jon for a second, then stretched himself upright. "I'm just gonna have a brew. Could yer use a cuppa?"

Jon could feel the cold. He had had nothing to eat or drink since he had got up. He found a word, "Yeah," and followed the man into the café. He might as well wait inside where he could sit down.

The old man cluttered about behind the counter while Jon sat and waited on a nearby table. He watched as the man dumped some teabags into a pot and found two mugs. Jon shut out the sounds.

Jon was aware that here he would not hear Bill, or his mother, or his teachers, or those girls whose very presence tormented him. Although he was sitting down he felt light, almost elevated. He sat upright and watched as the old man poured the tea and brought him a mugful.

"Sugar, mate?"

"Oh, er – yeah."

The man hovered near him as he supped his tea, concerned, but not like a mother. He watched, but said and did nothing. He was giving the boy his space, observing him with respect. Jon was totally unaware. The café was very still and quiet for the moment but the old man was expecting his first customer at any time now. He quietly stifled his anxiety, watching this stray boy, this embryonic man, and hoping that no one would arrive to upset the moment of calm. Soon the boy had finished his warm, sweet tea.

"'Nother one?"

"Yeah." The boy had to make an effort to hold back phrases he rarely used, phrases such as, *thank you* and, *not half*.

The man returned to the counter. This time he brought his own mug and sat to one side of the table. "So – lookin' for a job then?"

"Sort of."

"What kind of job?"

"Dunno. Somethin' that pays a bit. " Jon turned away from the questions and looked towards the door. More bloody questions again, but this was different. He knew that he couldn't make tea like this; he swallowed another mouthful.

"When did yer leave school, then?"

"I ain't, not yet. Soon, though."

"So it's a part-time job you want then, sort of Saturday job."

"Yeah."

"After school, perhaps?"

"Yeah, s'pose so."

Jon shifted uneasily on his chair – the bloke from the garage still hadn't come. What was this old geezer givin' him tea for? The old man didn't seem troubled by him, not like most of the old people he knew. He was a short stocky man, about sixty, Jon thought, but he noticed too the strong arms and the man's upright stance – he stood very square on strong legs, secure and steady. He was relaxed too – comfortable in his presence. That was what was odd about him – he wasn't bothered by him.

The old man watched him, saw him looking towards the door. Perhaps 'e thinks I might be some sort of pervert, perhaps 'e's worried that I'm gonna touch 'im up or something stupid like that. Funny little kid – all aggression one minute, swearing and carrying on, then supping his tea like a grateful old pensioner the next. Poor little sod. Look at the bloody state of him, scruffy, angry, bloody miserable. If I'd let my kids get like this the old woman would've killed me. He let the easy, natural flow of thought take him along. Where's 'e come from? What bastard's let him get into this state?

Somewhere close by a car came to a halt. Someone got out and slammed the door. The smell of bacon wafted over to Jon from the other side of the counter.

"That 'im?"

"Yeah. Sounds like his motor." Jon was getting to his feet.

"'Ang about. Give 'im a chance to get in." Jon paused. "'Ow about a bacon sandwich, then pop along to 'ave a word?" Jon sat down, but kept his eyes towards the door, like a dog, chained and waiting.

"There y'are then. Get yerself round that." Jon needed no further instruction; the sandwich soon vanished. "Now pop along to Paul's. Tell him I'll see him later."

Outside, Jon hesitated. What was he going to say? What sort of job did he want? What sort of job could he do? He almost frightened himself with these questions. They were not really his questions: they were Barry's or Steve's. It was only when he was just a few feet from the garage that they confronted him. He was struggling as some children struggle when summoned unexpectedly to a headteacher's office.

He looked into a dark place, a sort of dim cave. The rear of a light-coloured car threw back the early morning sunlight and he struggled to see beyond it. All he could make out was the confused jumble of a workbench and above that a wall that someone had painted white, years back. He stood in the doorway and an old Pirelli calendar, a pin-up from long ago, caught his eye. He moved closer. The girl looked straight at him but did not shout and scream. She had no friends with her so he stood and returned her stare.

"Not bad, is she? Doesn't show her age." The man was relaxed and starting to smile. "Now, what can I do for you, young man?"

"Me mate said yer might find me a job." The man smiled again. He was younger than the man at the café, and leaner looking too. He was too kind to laugh.

"What sort of job d'yer think I might 'ave for yer, then?" More fuckin' questions! The man watched his face, then Jon shifted slightly to one side. "What I mean is, I don't often have jobs for anybody here – I haven't the space, see." He nodded across the workshop and Jon's gaze followed. "'Ave yer left school yet? Yer might find a Saturday job round here somewhere, in the market perhaps, but I've nothing in that line." The man saw the immediate disappointment in the boy's face. "Who was this mate who sent yer? Anyone I know?"

"Barry I think 'is name is. Saw 'im in a pub last night."

"Oh Barry, yeah, I know who you mean. He was a right good'un, 'e was. Used to see to his old fellah's car. Asked me if I'd give 'im a Saturday job." The man remembered what Jon had just said. "Yeah, 'e was all right, was Barry. I used to get more work then." The man became curious. "What's 'e doing now, d'yer know?"

"Nah. Only met 'im last night."

"And 'e said I might find yer a job down 'ere?"

"Yeah." Jon waited for something more encouraging.

"Well, sorry to disappoint yer. Why don't yer try some other places round here?"

As he passed the café the old man was waiting outside. Around him there lingered the smell of bacon and the clinking of tea mugs.

"Well then. 'Ow d'yer get on?"

"What d'you wanna know for?"

"What d'yer mean?"

"There's no bloody job. Waste of fuckin' time!"

"There yer go again, all bloody swearin' and upsetting me customers." Fortunately, they did not look around at Jon. The old man stood in front of him and continued, "Listen, you were effin' and blindin' when you first came 'ere this morning. Yer got two mugs of tea and a bacon sandwich. D'yer think that swearin' at people's always gonna work like that? It 'asn't got you that job, 'as it?"

Jon wanted to knock this interfering old git out of the way but something held him back. He could sense his anger but also his own weakness in the face of the man's quiet determination. The old man watched as his frustration and anger started to loosen their grip. "I've got something you can do for me. Come and 'ave another sandwich first."

Jon hesitated, but the old man stood in his way and there was still the smell of bacon. For the second time that morning he followed the old man inside.

"Now then, while you're eatin' this, I'll get Paul's breakfast. You can take 'is tray along. Show 'im 'ow useful you are, see, get talkin', like. Go back again, let 'im see you're all right, see?" The old man had seen the start of a scowl on Jon's face. "Yeah, I know, you're not a bleedin' waiter, but that's not the point. Paul doesn't know bugger all about you, does he? So why should 'e take any notice of you unless you can show him you're not just some useless kid?"

The bacon sandwich tasted good, really good. For once Jon had too much in his mouth to be unpleasant and he had to listen. He was trapped by a good breakfast, and he was feeling a bit unsure of himself. Why was this silly old git bothering about him like this? He was fussing worse than a whole bunch of teachers, but he could cook! And Jon's mouth was stuffed full of bacon sandwich so he had to stay. He wasn't very sure about taking the tray over to the garage, but there was another sandwich to finish – the old man had seen to that.

"It's like me old man said – 'e fought in the First World War, yer know – when I left school." Another mug of sweet tea had appeared on the table. "Yeah, there weren't no jobs then and I'd left school at fourteen – couldn't wait to leave the place, bloody teachers and their straps and their canes." For a moment Jon stopped eating and looked up. "No dole neither, nor bloody family allowance. Nothin'! Anyway, just before I left, 'e said, 'It's like this, boy, you've gotta pay yer way. You've gotta get a job. Get lookin' around. Don't be fussy about what you have to do to start with, just get a job, any job.' What 'e explained was, once I'd got a job and proved meself a bit, there was a chance I could find something better. It didn't always work like that, but it improved yer chances." He looked straight at Jon. "You don't look the type to come round lookin' for jobs. 'Ow keen are yer? 'Ow badly d'yer need one?"

"Dunno. Money'd be useful, like."

"Hmmm. Think about it while you take this lot over to Paul." There wasn't much on the tray, just a large, over-filled mug and a plate loaded with eggs and bacon and some thickly-cut slices of bread. Jon was not used to carrying a tray like this and was aware of the customers watching him. He grasped each end of it so tightly and nervously that his arms locked rigid and he could not turn around properly to see where he was going. He took two steps like a stiff-legged puppet and caught his foot on the leg of a table. Some of the tea surged out of the mug, just missing the plate and slopping onto the tray. Jon forgot to bring the tray up level so the tea gathered speed and cascaded onto a pair of boots.

"Jaysus!" The Irish voice was a friendly one. "It's as well Old

Jimmy fills'em right up." He turned to his mates. "Let the man through, fellahs." His mates laughed and made an easy passage for the boy.

"Hey Jimmy, are we all gonna get waiter service now?" The others laughed again. This time Jon caught the man's eye and he smiled in spite of himself. At last, he piloted the tray through the door. For a moment the old man thought that he was about to watch the collapse of a balancing act – the boy was not very well co-ordinated.

"What, you again? Oh, you've brought me breakfast. You bin talkin' to Old Jimmy, 'ave yer?" The man stood there wiping a large spanner. "Just put it down there, will yer? Thanks."

The tea swirled around again in the mug and the eggs and bacon slid across the plate, just stopping at the edge of the tray. There was a small, unoccupied space on the bench where Jon could slide the tray in amongst the bits and pieces. The Pirelli girl watched them.

"Old Jimmy's not found you a job, 'as 'e?"

"Nah. 'E just asked me to bring this over."

"That's good of yer." Jon felt embarrassed and slightly confused. He rarely received thanks for anything. He was beginning to feel trapped in this strange, unfamiliar world. The man rescued him:"'Ad a job before?"

"Nah."

"Hmmm. That's the trouble, see. Everyone'll ask yer that. They want to know that you can make yerself useful, not have to be told what to do all the time." He waved towards the chaos that was his workshop. "There's a lot to keep straight 'ere – I have to be very organised, yer know." The man stopped himself and hoped that the boy would not realise that he had come close to offering him some work. He had noticed something about the boy but he was unsure.

Jon was shifting towards the door. A second dose of friendliness was more than he could take this morning.

"You off, then?"

"Yeah."

"See yer, then. Thanks for bringing me grub over."

Only as he made his way up the road did Jon find his thoughts returning again to school, his home and Bill. He was aware that at last he was leaving something behind.

Chapter Eight

On Sunday morning Jon was eating cornflakes in the kitchen when his mother came in. She put her keys down near a cupboard and picked up the kettle.

"Oh, there you are. Where the bleedin' 'ell did yer get to yesterday?" The boy continued to eat his cornflakes, sucking noisily on the spoon. "Yer didn't tell me you were going anywhere."

"Just went out."

His mother started to speak again just as the next spoonful reached his mouth. "Can't you eat quiet?" He took another mouthful. The flakes were dry this time and he crunched them energetically and with great satisfaction. Soon the bowl was empty.

"Who yer bin with?"

"Dunno – just out, like."

"Well there's some more nosy bleeders want to know about yer. This came yesterday." She snatched up a slip of paper from the side. "You've bin bunkin' off school again, you little fool. Look!" She waved the paper in his face. "They're gonna to take me to court 'cos of you!"

He retreated to the corner of the kitchen. If she'd been one of the girls from school he would have shoved her out of the way. She was about the same build. The girls at school were just like her – in your face, aggressive, yelling things at you, coming at you, daring you to stand your ground, knowing you wouldn't, bullying you with their eyes and their mouths and their bodies. But somehow it was different with her.

"Are you bleedin' listenin'?" Her anger poured out into the room and swept over her son. "Why I ever had you, I'll never know – always in bloody trouble, bloody neighbours on about you pinching things, and teachers. Always up the school for some bloody reason, right from the start – should 'ave done what Carol said and got you adopted, got rid of you." The paper in his mother's hand was now reduced to a tight ball and she threw it viciously towards the sink. Jon watched the ball of paper fall short, and laughed nervously.

"That's right, bloody well laugh, that's all you're good for, you never take any notice. You ask them out there – you know what they say about you? They wanna know why I put up with all this shit." His mother kicked at the ball of paper which had come to rest just in front of her. It slid over to her son who ignored it; the urge to kick it back was strong but now was not the time. Jon kept very still.

Why didn't he say something, do something? Why didn't he respond, get back at her – she could see him in front of her, her own flesh and blood, but her anger just went straight through him. She resented his ability to let her words pass him by. So much energy expended, yet he was still unscathed – she could not touch him. "God, you make me so bloody angry – can't you ever take any notice?"

That was the last thing he wanted to do. He wanted to escape, even away to the girls at school. It was not difficult, with his mother screeching at him. With them, you could shut your eyes and barge past, make the quick fleeting contact and then escape, perhaps with a moment's brushed pleasure on the way; he thought of the girl in the pub doorway.

"What the 'ell am I gonna do about this?" The paper jumped up and down in front of his face.

"Dunno."

But he was beginning to mould an answer, not one that he could reveal, not one that he wanted to reveal – she'd go spare if she found out. There'd be more of her questions and now he was desperate to answer his own. He realised that she'd never helped and it was too late to ask her now. She turned away from him, shoved down the switch on the kettle then lit another cigarette. Jon sat down, wearily.

Yes, she was like the girls at school; she was always there and her questions had no sell-by dates, did not fade away into the air, and sometimes could reach uncomfortably far back into the past. She looked tired, and for once he wondered where she had been. He was aware of one or two men but, apart from one who had been part of their household for a while, he had not known any of them. Norm, it had been, Uncle Norm who had been around one Christmas – he'd come to fetch him home from school, from the infants. The man had stood alone outside the school gates, away from the mums and the older girls who were waiting. For a second Jon recalled one or two of the girls, older sisters and cousins of his classmates who, he now realised, should themselves have been in school. Then the realisation that they too had had their reasons for not bothering to go there was a comfort, a reassurance to him.

Yes, for a while, touching their lives, but not part of them, there had been this man, Norm, who was tall and thin. Jon had felt uncertain about this familiar yet unknown acquaintance who existed alongside him. At first he thought that Norm must just have been passing by, as at that stage in his life uncles so often seemed to do. That was what an uncle did, it was all part of a man's function to go out and look at women – he knew that from the few times when he had been able to watch television with them, or read over their shoulders, and that's what Norm was doing now. Apart from this sort of look-out function Norm seemed to have little reason to be outside school. He didn't notice Jon until he was standing right in front of him. "Hi Uncle Norm. What yer doin' 'ere?"

"Oh, there you are." The man looked up again and over to the other side of the gate.

"Bin 'ere long then, Uncle Norm?"

"Nah. We'll go in a minute."

"What a' we waiting for, Uncle Norm?"

The man turned to him now. "Just wait here a sec, will yer? Just hold on to this for me." Jon found himself clutching a folded copy of The Sun.

The group of women opened up as Norm approached. He spoke to one of them while the others stood and watched. Jon could see that they liked him because they all smiled, except for the one he was talking to. Soon Norm returned. There was no sign of his mother and Jon was used to this. He needed little encouragement to follow Norm, who studied his paper. He would soon be home.

But now this memory was too distant, and fading fast. What had Norm done for a job? Did he ever have a job?

****

The kettle boiled and his mother turned again to fill a solitary cup. Jon slipped past her and went up to his room.

Bill and school; for a moment he thought about them both. He could stay indoors today if the old woman didn't make his life hell, but if he went out to get away from her there was the chance of meeting Bill. He was every-bloody-where. He wondered about the court business. The old woman was doing her pieces about that, but Steve and that other bloke had said don't bother, play yer cards right and nothing will 'appen. Sod it, why should he bother with anything? He tried the old television in the corner of his room, but the sound had gone and the picture was none too good either. The other television was downstairs.

No, there were no answers at home, never had been and never would be. He grabbed his jacket and left the house.

He was soon hungry again. Outside, the air was warm but the warmth only penetrated him slowly. He remained hunched up, as if he were still cold from the house. He looked like someone carrying something precious, something he would fight to keep.

The chippy was closed and there were few people around. Jon found himself outside a parkland area on the edge of town. It was somewhere he had never visited before, well away from his home. For a while he sat on a swing, moving himself back and forward with little effort. A couple with young children came along and stared hard at him. He left the swing to them and their kids and found a bench at the edge of the play area. One end of the bench was clear of rubbish so he sat there for a few moments, wondering what to do next.

Someone there had been eating a Chinese take-away. The strong sunshine was warming the rubbish and the smell of the food reached him. He leant along the bench and rummaged through the greasy bags and aluminium containers. Then he stood up and moved to the bin at the other end of the bench. The couple were occupied with their children. He moved an old newspaper from the top of the bin and started to explore the remains of the meal. All he found was some sweet and sour pork nestling in crumpled foil. He hesitated, then stuffed it quickly into his mouth and sat down again. He noticed the couple watch him for a moment and he felt uncomfortable.

The little girl made her way over to him. She stood in front of him and waved a doll in one hand, waiting for his inspection and approval. She was about three and had a child's wonderful self-assurance. She was warmly dressed with a plaid skirt that he could just see below a bright woollen jacket. Her black patent leather shoes were secured by wide velcro straps. Jon watched her, his attention held by this tiny spark of life.

Somewhere in the background he could hear the other child crying and noticed that both parents were attending to the little boy. The woman was stroking his forehead with one hand and pulling him close to her with the other. The man carefully undid one of the pockets of a bag that hung from a pushchair and retrieved something for the woman.

When the little girl called out Jon turned to see her pointing to her doll which had fallen into a puddle. It was a large doll, almost as tall as the little girl. Face down it lay with its yellow plaits sloping into the filthy water like mooring ropes. The parents had not heard and the girl started to cry, pointing at the doll. Jon stood up. The girl was wailing now, pointing to the doll and wailing, one hand up to her face. Automatically, Jon bent down and rescued the doll.

The wailing ceased and was replaced by a sniffing and snuffling which convulsed the little girl's frame and troubled her pretty face. Jon held out the doll to the girl but she would not approach and her brother was still holding his parents' attention. With his free hand, Jon beckoned to the girl. After a few moments' hesitation she moved towards him, her eyes fixed on the doll.

The man looked up. "Oh, poor Lucy. What happened to her then?" The little girl ran straight back to him and started to cry again. Jon held out the doll.

"Come on then, what's the matter?" the man asked, but there was no reply through the sobbing. For a moment or two the girl shook as she pulled herself into her father's embrace and he gripped her tightly with one arm.

"She dropped it in the puddle." The man looked at Jon quizzically. "She wouldn't take it back off me. It's just a bit wet, like."

"Er, no she wouldn't – you know what little girls are like." The man seemed more relaxed now – for a moment he had been anxious to know what had made his daughter cry.

The little boy was quiet now and his mother turned to the

others. She looked Jon up and down and then looked across to the bench and the mess where he had been. For a moment she was not sure what to think or say. Then she stood up and took the doll from Jon's hand, all in one swift movement as if he were about to take off with it. He backed away from this determined female. There was a moment of perfume and softness and then the hardness looked back at him from behind the man.

The man was embarrassed. He stood up, holding the little girl's hand. "Thanks for picking it up." He tried to smile at Jon whose unease was clear. "Yeah – thanks," he added. Jon could see that he meant it. The woman called to the man and they moved away.

Jon was soon hungry again. There was a van just outside the park where people were queuing for ice creams and hot dogs but he had no money and most of the children had adults with them. There would be no treats from other kids. He was also aware that he was off his patch so he had to be more careful about the chances he took here. He passed two little girls struggling with huge hot dogs. The girls weren't much bigger than the little girl with the doll but he turned away from them and set off for home.

He arrived without incident, just after two. The house was empty and he was relieved that his mother was not there to bother him again. He snatched open the fridge door and the doors of the kitchen cupboards. What little food there was he slammed down on the worktop. Only the baked beans were of interest. He remembered the freezer compartment of the fridge and looked in there. Frozen vegetarian pie. Stuff it. He found a tin opener near the toaster and took a spoon from a drawer. In the next room he switched on the television, sat down on the sofa and attacked the tin. At his first attempt the opener slipped and he nearly gashed a lump out of his hand. He leaned forward and rested the tin on the low table. For a moment he took his eyes off the screen. The opener slipped again and this time half the contents of the tin turned themselves out onto the flat surface.

"Bleedin' thing!" For a brief moment he hesitated while something caught his eye on the screen then, with his left hand, he pushed the cold beans onto the spoon and swallowed them. When he had emptied the tin he was both hungry still and uncomfortable. The television held him only for a few moments before he got up and went upstairs to his mother's room.

The door was open and the curtains had not been drawn back. He hesitated, peered through the uncertain gloom, then went in. He was hungry and took little notice of what he disturbed as he looked in all the usual places for money. His search became increasingly frantic until he found a few pounds which had been forgotten.

Later, when he returned home, he had eaten a great deal and was carrying further supplies. He dumped these in the kitchen and returned to the television. He was still there when his mother arrived. He was aware of her turning the key and stepping into the hall. For a moment she did not close the door behind her and he thought he heard heavier steps follow her into the house. He listened closely while his mother ran up the stairs. He could hear her cursing up in her room where the sound of her voice was punctuated by the slamming of wardrobe doors. Jon dismissed the sounds of her anger and tried to listen to whatever was out in the hall – he did not want to reveal himself until he knew who was there.

Suddenly his mother was running back down the stairs and straight into the living room. The door into the hallway remained open behind her.

"What sort of bleedin' stunt 'ave you pulled now, you little sod? What d'yer mean, goin' through my bleedin' room like that? Thought you'd find some money, did yer, you rotten little thief? Well, yer didn't find much, did yer?" Wearily he glared back at her and tried to fight her words. His mother continued. "I really know what you're like now, don't I?"

The man stood in the doorway. He was taller than Jon and thicker set. Jon took one step towards the door and stopped. The man had not moved a muscle.

"This thieving little swine is my son. I don't know why he has to steal from me. He can piss off out of here right now for all I care." The man watched Jon closely and eased himself off the doorframe. Jon's mother stepped towards the man and Jon thought she was going to push him back into the hall but, instead of seizing the man and dragging him to one side, his mother slowed, turned her shoulder gently into his and leant against him. Then she stood there, folding her arms across her chest, and held forth.

There was no other way out of the living room so Jon had to

endure the torrent of abuse. Its initial force carried him along the table to the fridge where he was able to escape some of the blast. His mother shouted and harangued him but, for once, did not step towards him – he had fairly recent memories of the thin arms belabouring him, the short woman breathing heavily and the angry, futile words flung at him between gasps. There was none of that now. He sensed that his mother was almost enjoying herself, was letting go and saying things that she had longed to say and had been saving up for years. As she screamed and shouted, she eased herself away from the man and stood slightly apart from him, shaking with rage. The man did not move and waited for her to lean back again.

Within him, something turned. He had meant to wait until his mother had finished before he tried to leave but he knew that he could put up with her noise no longer. He knew that if he listened to any more of her insults and anger he would start to feel them. He took two further steps around the table, grabbed his jacket and walked to the door. Suddenly, his mother stopped. Embarrassed now, the stranger moved back into the hall and the woman fell back against him. Jon's eyes caught the man's as he swept past him, and then he was out of the door. For a moment Jon looked back and noticed the man's arm laid across his mother's shoulder.

Round the corner Jon stopped and enjoyed the sense of relief. For a moment, strangely, he felt a little sympathy for his mother. Somehow, in spite of her fury, she had seemed frail and helpless. He couldn't say why exactly, but somehow in all that screaming and abuse, it was as if she had been screaming at herself. She had shaken with sheer frustration and her torrent of words seemed to weigh her down, to weaken her, even with that man standing behind her. Jon knew he was all right – he had got away from it all; it was his mother who seemed trapped.

The memory of the young father in the park came back to him. He remembered the alarm on the man's face and wondering whether the man was going to hit him because his daughter was crying. He remembered the man cuddling the little girl and her quietly sobbing into his shoulder. What was this cuddling business? Thoughts of the girls from school, the girls in the pub and his mother made him feel uncomfortable. He remembered the man's arm around his mother's shoulder and scenes he had seen on television of couples in bed. No way, not his mother, she was bloody ancient, poor old cow.

He began to realise then what he had to do. It was as if the man at home had given him a little push, some momentum that would move him along. With his silent presence, the man had underlined his mother's helplessness, her inability to do anything with her son. Somehow, Jon glimpsed an important truth about himself and discovered a spark of resolve, a resolve not to be messed about by her any more. He contemplated school with the same resolve, where the hollowness of official sympathy was so obvious to him. He didn't need anything explained and no adult had ever encouraged him to trust his own judgement like this. Jon simply had an overwhelmingly powerful feeling that he had had enough and that adults in general were no longer going to piss him about.

Then he remembered Bill. It was Sunday and there was no school, no job-hunting. He looked around and moved on.

Chapter Nine

His mother woke him on Monday. Before she spoke, she wrenched open the curtains, flooding the room with light. For a moment she had the upper hand again. "Right, it's school time so up yer get. Come on, I'm not 'aving any more bother 'cos of you!"

He resisted the urge to shout at her, to drive her out of his room with his anger. He tried to turn over away from the light and her noise, but she seized a corner of the bedclothes and his warmth was gone.

There was nowhere left where he could snuggle down so he climbed out in his odd mixture of underwear, T-shirt and a sock. There was no sympathy for his mother this morning. For a moment he thought he was going to hit her. Instead he brushed her aside and went into the bathroom. Behind the door he listened to her shouting at him and then he heard her go downstairs. He knew that her interest in him would not last. Eventually, however, he did set off for school.

Mrs. Lambert looked up when he answered at registration time, but she said nothing. It was Tracey who welcomed him. "Hi Jon - nice and early today! No thievin' to do?" The others laughed.

The teacher's voice droned on with the list of names and Jon turned to a quieter boy sitting near him. "What's first lesson then?"

"Maths, I think."

"Shit!"

The other kids were no bother. They trailed out of the room and into the corridor, then Mrs. Lambert stood between him and the door. There was no pushing her out of the way. "I'm free this lesson so you and I had better try and sort out this attendance business." Jon said nothing. "Is there any chance of getting hold of your mother this morning?"

"Dunno."

"Is she at work?"

"Dunno." This time he watched her. He tried to imagine her with a man's arm around her shoulder. She noticed the hint of a smile light across his face.

"There's nothing funny when you don't even know where your parents are." Again he was silent. The trace of a smile would not go – he would play her along. He sensed her growing frustration and, for once, he was almost enjoying her interrogation. He smiled again when she announced that they would have to see Mr. Fisher.

"So, you've told Mrs. Lambert that you don't know where your mother is? Come on Jon, where is she?" Old Fisher had begun.

"Dunno."

"That's no answer, Jon. Come on, we've been through all this before."

So, it was all matey this morning, was it? Silly old sod. Doesn't he realise what a prat he is?

"Well Sir, she goes off to work in the morning and I don't see no more of her till the evening."

"But Jon, I need to get hold of her. Does she still work at the same place?"

There was a knock at the door. Jon recognised the face of the man who had knocked at the house a few days before. He had not expected to see the attendance officer so soon. "Good morning, Mr. Fisher." The man paused. "Good morning. Er, Jon, isn't it?" He continued looking at Jon, but spoke to the teacher. "Good job I was in this morning, wasn't it?" He smiled at both of them. The teacher rustled some papers. "Now what are we going to do about this young man then, Mr. Fisher?"

The rustling stopped. The teacher produced a collection of papers, neatly clipped together, flipped them across his desk to the other man and nodded to him.

"Quite a record, isn't it?" Jon said nothing while the attendance officer leafed through the papers. "Worst I've seen for a while."

Mr. Fisher nodded again, then looked back to Jon. "Do you realise, Jon, that every instance of your truancy is recorded here? Every time you've bunked off, that fact has been recorded. If Mr. Knowles here has to start court proceedings, all this will be used. It's worrying, isn't it?"

"Dunno." What did he expect him to say? Despite the pressure he remembered Steve saying that it would be his old woman who'd be taken to court, who'd be fined, if ever things got that far. They'd have to find her first. He decided to sit it out. He had learnt this ploy long ago and the months and years of truancy had slid gently by.

"I really am giving you a very last chance." Mr. Knowles had finished leafing through the papers. Mr. Fisher was now holding them in one hand and tapping them with the back of his other hand. He was still looking at the other man and Jon was impatient to get away. All he wanted to do was to escape from these two prats and get on with the week. He was thinking of Bill when Mr. Fisher coughed and stared at him. "I don't think you're even listening, are you Jon?"

This time Jon could not be bothered. Stupid bastard, what does he think I'm doing? He thought of Steve this time and inside he felt the worm of anger at work. He had some questions to put and he wondered what Steve would say now.

"Well, what you've got to face is this. Each time you truant from now on, I'll phone Mr. Knowles here and within a very short time you'll find yourself in court. Apart from what that'll mean for you," – here Jon almost laughed out loud – "it'll cause your mum no end of trouble and upset." Jon had a fleeting vision of his mother shouting at him about lost wages and losing her job. "So, what are you going to do about it, then?"

"'Ave ter see, won't I?" He was pleased with the expression on the teacher's face but before Mr. Fisher could reply, Jon remembered the need to play along. "Bit more effort like, I suppose."

"Could you explain, Jon?"

"Well, come and say 'ello to yer, first thing in the morning." For a moment he felt daring. "Let yer know I've arrived safely, like." He thought of the few occasions when he had been in school first thing in the morning. He remembered the kids swirling all over the place, in and out of offices and toilets and the classrooms. No one ever knew what was going on at that time of the day.

"I think that's an excellent idea, don't you, Mr. Knowles?"

"Fine, just what we want."

The stupid prats were nodding at each other again, like two parrots he had seen once on the television. It was hard not to smile.

"You'd best be off to class then, but remember what we've said."

Jon wondered whether he would make it to lunchtime. He was entitled to free lunch vouchers but he had never bothered to work out how to get them, and the food was crap anyway. Better to look for friends near the chippy. Then, once he had smiled again at Old Fisher he would have finished his school day and could see what the afternoon would bring. He couldn't remember where to go for a P.E. lesson which came next, but then another boy from his class appeared and he followed him.

"Where's your kit, then?"

"Dunno, Sir."

"Whatcha mean, don't know?" For a moment his own honesty had caught Jon out. "You don't know? 'Ow the 'ell can we do P.E. if we don't know where our kit is?"

"Left it in the cloakroom. Can I just pop and get it, Sir?" Jon was doing well this morning – none of your vague, "Left it somewhere". Jon was discovering the power of words.

"Go on then, be quick."

Near the cloakrooms a small boy turned into the toilets. As he was leaving, he found Jon standing in front of him. He went to duck past Jon's outstretched arm, but Jon was ready for him. "Sold all them things yet? I bet you 'ave." His victim said nothing. "Well, let's see what you've got in your pockets, then." For a moment he thought that the boy was going to resist, but he must have sensed Jon's growing self-assurance. Jon left with a few more pounds in his back pocket and set off to see whether there were any stray items of P.E. kit lying around. There were none.

"Somebody must 'ave stolen me kit, Sir. I've looked all over for it."

"See me after the lesson – just sit over by the door until the bell goes." When the bell rang Jon had already gone.

After the lunch bell, Jon paused outside Mr.Fisher's office. For once he waited. At last the man arrived. He waved at Jon, who stepped across his path, then turned into the room. Jon headed for the chippy.

He paid for his chips and set off towards home. Further along the girls waited and he noticed an uncertain air about them; there were only three of them and he realised that one of them was missing. "Where's old cow-face then?"

The gang seemed incomplete without Tracey but her deputy stepped forward: "None a' your bleedin' business!" Jon tried to stuff the remains of his chip papers into the crook of her arm but she turned and the rubbish fell to the ground. Jon walked on past the old car which now stood in the new grass.

He did little that afternoon. Just before the end of afternoon school he walked again past Mr. Fisher's office and made sure that the teacher saw him. He had actually spent two hours in lessons, more than he had for some time, but by break the following morning he had had enough. Mr. Fisher had actually smiled at him that morning. Jon arrived on time and met him near his room. Mr. Fisher's schoolteacher-smile troubled Jon, but he smiled back without revealing his contempt for the man. At registration he faced the form for the second time that week.

"Bleedin' keen today, aren't yer?"

"Back already – what's up with yer Jon?"

"Yer fancy her, don't yer?" Lisa leered while Tracey grinned her approval.

"Course he fancies her – 'aven't yer noticed how he looks at her?"

"Piss off, you old slag." Jon sat with his head down and tried to ignore the girls.

" I think we ought to warn Miss about him."

"Yeah, she ain't safe on 'er own with 'im. She's always trying to chat him up."

"Still, 'e don't bother us, though – noisy lot, ain't we –not good enough for 'im."

"Naah. He'd only fancy a teacher."

"Yeah, little teacher's pet."

Of all the kids in the class, Tracey was the one who could really needle Jon. She could never leave him alone, just like his mother. Around him, shouts and screams rose up until Mrs. Lambert entered the room. Tracey turned to speak to her immediately and Jon wondered what was coming. "Look, Miss, Jon's back already – he must like it round 'ere." There was more jeering, but Jon allowed the girl her moment and her audience.

He found himself behind a group of boys, away from Mrs. Lambert. Mrs. Lambert tried to settle the girls, then turned to the boys. "Oh, Jon. You're here again. That's nice." The girls cat-called and Jon was on his feet again. "Sit down please, Jon. It's not lesson time yet." He sat, slowly and reluctantly. Silly cow. What did she want to keep him here for with this lot of tossers? As soon as the bell rang he had gone.

A double lesson of science was too much, the first science lesson he had attended for three weeks. The teacher moved in and out of the room next door and Jon chose his moment to leave. None of the other kids troubled themselves about his going. Near the back entrance someone had left a bike and Jon rode it out of the yard.

A car blared its horn at him and the driver swerved violently. Another car slowed for a moment, lights flashing. Jon made it to the next turning and paused. In front of him was half a mile of downhill and by the time he had reached the bottom he felt some confidence. Another ten minutes and he found himself outside the café opposite Paul's garage. It was not where he had intended to be; he had just arrived. The café was open, but there was no sign of the old man. Jon wheeled the bike towards the garage. A small door was open and beyond it was the oily gloom of the garage.

Somehow he could not go in, could not bring himself to trespass on this private world of men. The pub had been different, somewhere where both men and women went, where anybody and everybody could go in and out as they pleased. Here, these men were stuck fast and chose to operate alone. They were happy and this both puzzled and disturbed Jon.

Why? Why come down here every day and get covered in grease, mending cars? Why did he enjoy his work? Jon moved off down the road and sat slumped against a wall in the sunshine. Beyond the garage and the line of railway arches he could see a clock. He thought of lunchtime at school and his intention to see Mr. Fisher again. Then the two men appeared outside the garage and started to make their way across to the café. Old Jimmy saw him first.

"Wotcha mate! 'Ow yer doin', then?" The men waited outside the café for him to join them.

He remembered to stand the bike up against the kerb where it could be seen; didn't want it nicked. It was turning out useful.

"Cuppa tea then, mate?" Jon nodded. "Day off school, is it?" Jon said nothing. "Sit down 'ere, next to old Paul. 'Es 'avin' a mornin' off an' all, I reckon." Paul smiled at Jon but spoke to Jimmy.

"I wouldn't stay away from school with all them girls there – you'd never get me away from the place. Got any favourites?"

"They're all crap!"

"Really?" Paul grinned. "No wonder you're bunkin' off. Nothin' else there, I suppose." For a moment, Jon remembered Mr. Fisher and the need to convince him that he had been at school. He smelt bacon and decided to stay put.

Jimmy put two mugs on the table and went back for his own. When he returned he was also carrying a plate of bacon sandwiches. He put them down between Paul and Jon then picked up a sandwich for himself.

"Don't suppose they miss you when you're not in school, do they?" Jimmy was busy with his sandwich. "You know, they don't bother too much, do they? They didn't in my day." Both men laughed. "I know you're supposed to worry about exams these days, but you can get round that." Jon was beginning to feel uncomfortable. He needed some words, but the right ones would not come. He got to his feet.

"Where you off to now, back to those girls then?"

"Nah. Gotta report in or I'll get into bother."

"What will you do when you've reported in? Do they make you go to classes then?"

"Depends, like." They waited for him to continue. "Some classes ain't too bad, but they're mostly crap." He paused again. He didn't know what to make of these questions; it was as if they wanted to contaminate themselves with the wrong part of his life. It was a part that did not belong to them. "Gotta go." Some of the new words returned. "Thanks for the tea." He was halfway back to school before he remembered the bike.

He looked up, saw the sign for the hospital and remembered Steve. He knew that he wanted to see him. There was still no job and he'd got to get away from school and his mother as well as that bastard brother of Dean's. Steve was just going off duty when Jon met him in the outpatients area.

"All right then, Jon? 'Ow yer doing?"

"All right." The universal lie.

"What yer doin' 'ere, then? Want a coffee?"

The hospital cafeteria was stuffy and noisy, but it was anonymous.

"What did you rush out of the pub for last week? What happened?"

Jon thought for a moment. "Dunno."

"What d'yer mean?"

"All those fuckin' questions."

"Old Barry was right though – you can't just walk into a job." They paused and drank. "Did you try that place he told you about, you know, down by the railway?"

"Yeah."

"How did you get on?"

"Crap – no bleedin' job."

"What did they say, then?"

"Not a lot. There was some old man in a café gave me a cup of tea. Funny old sod – 'e didn't give a toss what I said to him."

"What about the garage?"

"Nah, nothin' there. The bloke was all right, but no bleedin' job."

"Why don't you do what Barry said, hang about the place a bit, get your face known?"

"Been down there this mornin'. Nicked a bike and left it down there."

"What did you go down there for, then?"

"I couldn't stand bleedin' school, not all that crap. I signed in with Old Fisher but science … " Jon was genuinely uncomfortable at the thought of a science lesson. He got a grip on himself. "Not bleedin' likely. Then I pinched the bike."

"Want a sarnie?" Steve was getting to his feet.

"Yeah, okay."

Steve waited in the queue and left Jon to sit alone. The boy had tolerated a stream of questions and had not stormed off. He had also returned to the two men who had not offered him jobs and had left a bike there.

And Jon, what did he make of all this? No job but they were all right somehow and – he wasn't very sure about this – perhaps there was a chance. He knew with all the certainty of a frightened child that he did not want to explore anywhere else. For the moment he knew that he could not cope any more with the unfamiliar or the unknown.

"Well then. What yer gonna do about the bike?"

"What d'yer mean?" The sandwich was already in Jon's hand.

"It sounds like a decent bike." Steve had already decided that this was not the moment to tackle the business of theft. "You gonna fetch it back?"

"S'pose so."

"Could be useful, gettin' around, lookin' for jobs."

"It didn't 'alf shift!" Jon remembered the air rushing past, all the way down to the railway arches.

"Well then, nip down and get it back. Let them see you again, let them think they know you, let them think you're all right."

"I'll go and get it in the mornin', after break."

Then there would be no need to go to maths. It gave him a sense of importance, as if he were making appointments and organising his own time. He thought of the afternoon bell at school.

"Better go – gotta clock in again."

"Busy man, then. You coming down the pub this week? I'll be there Thursday, 'bout nine."

"Reckon so." This time he meant it. He stood up. "Cheers then."

He joined the other kids, drifting back into the school, and found some boys from the same class. With them he shuffled in and sat down. Mrs. Lambert cleared her throat, called the register then made an announcement.

"Jonathan, I contacted your mother this morning." There were mock gasps and jeers from the girls. "She's coming in to see Mr. Fisher and me."

"You're in the shit now, mate!" The boy next to him was always encouraging.

Mrs. Lambert glared; it was difficult to get the boy alone to tell him things like this. "Jonathan, you'd better wait behind."

He was not surprised that they had contacted his mother, although when he did turn up to lessons it was clear that some of the teachers didn't even know his name. His mother coming up to school, that was what really surprised him. That he couldn't believe.

"We had to insist – she's very cross." Jon smiled at the thought of his mother shouting at Mr. Fisher. "I don't think it's very funny, Jon." Mrs. Lambert glared at him. "This is very serious now." Embarrassed by her growing anger, he turned away so that she could no longer see his smile. He sensed her focus, her confidence, her determination; she was at him again, seizing on his lack of words, and he hated it. Why couldn't she leave him alone? What made her go on bothering him?

"Look Jon, she's got to be told. You're in terrible trouble if we don't sort this out – you're too young not to be in school." He sensed a pause and wondered what would come next. He wondered how she would keep the flow of words coming. It was like being out in showery rain – you never knew whether it had really stopped. It was a lot of bollocks anyway – he had heard most of it before. But the thought of the old woman coming up from home, that bothered him.

"You're only fifteen and you're very young." She was still trying to get his attention. "Anyway, the law says that you must come to school, so that's it. Doesn't that bother you?" Jon glared, but remained silent, scared now of saying too much. "Aren't you bothered at the thought of going to court?"

"Dunno."

Jon appreciated the word; it was always a good, reliable way of shutting the bastards up. He smiled to himself.

Mrs. Lambert picked up her register and some papers. "Well, Jon, I suppose I'll see you tomorrow." She waited until he had left the room, as if she knew something of which Jon was unaware.

Chapter Ten

Outside it was raining so Jon decided to stay in school. It was not easy; there was maths.

"Where's old Whitey, then?" A young substitute for Mr. White had presented himself.

"Sit down please, I've got some work for you."

"What d'yer say yer name was, Blackie?"

"I said I wanted you to sit down. I've got some ..."

There was a crash at the back of the room. "Give me my bleedin' bag back, you fuckin' twat!" Tracey was towering over one of the smaller boys. He flung the bag towards another boy, a larger, well-built lad who clung to it possessively. The girl turned on him.

"Will you sit down?" No one heard the teacher. They did not want to hear the teacher. They had already decided that there was no prospect of learning anything much in this lesson, even if they wanted to. Whatever their good intentions, whatever the promises made by a few of them to their parents, they knew that they were trapped. Nothing useful was going to get done. Why not enjoy themselves, impress their classmates?

Jon had no friends in the class. The second boy saw him and looked for another boy to pass the bag to. None of them were in range so the bag reached Jon.

"Don't let the old slag get it!" someone shouted, for she had nearly reached Jon. Another boy held out his hands, eager for the pass but the clasp on the bag had come undone and its contents had spread themselves across the desks and onto the floor. Carefully, Jon turned the bag upside down. He shook it sharply, to make sure it was empty, then tossed it back to the girl. He decided that he could reach the door before the teacher, and left the room.

He passed Old Fisher's room as lessons were changing again. The man was on the phone and waved to Jon. As the other kids drifted or scrambled into the last lesson of the afternoon Jon found himself outside the back gates. He also found Bill.

"All right, young Jon? What yer doin' 'ere, then?" A friendly arm had already found its way around Jon's shoulder. Bill didn't want an answer to this question so he continued, "So why ain'tcha been round with that dosh, then?" This question did require an answer. Jon ducked and twisted. The man grasped at the boy's shoulder but it was gone and Jon was back inside the playground, aware now that he was being followed.

He tried to lose Bill around the corridors, making sure that he did not enter any dead-ends, but his pursuer advanced confidently, as if he had a right to be there.

A teacher stopped Jon for a moment. "Why are you out of class?"

"Gotta see Mr. Fisher." Bill came round the corner and Jon was off again. Bill paused.

"Excuse me, can I help?" The words of the teacher were lost on Bill who turned and walked quickly back towards the rear gate.

This time Old Fisher was not on the phone. "Ah, Jonathan, need a word with you." For once, Jon was happy to stay; it was important that Old Fisher knew what a hard time he had in school.

Slowly he faced the teacher. "That bloke, the one what thumped me the other week, 'es trying to follow me around school."

"You mean the man who assaulted you?"

"Yeah."

"He's in school now?"

"Yeah, down the corridor."

"Just stay here for a moment. Which way did he go?"

"Along past the labs, Sir."

Old Fisher was soon back, flustered.

"Did yer catch 'im, Sir?"

"No, no. You didn't get a better look at him this time, did you?"

"Not really – sort of big, like – dark hair and jeans."

"Are you quite sure it was the same man?"

"Oh yes."

"Did anyone else see him, d'yer know?"

"Er Miss, er whatsername, the new teacher, she saw him."

"You mean Miss Grant? I'll speak to her later. Anyway, there's something else I need to talk to you about." He waved Jon to a chair. The boy paused and looked towards the door. "Come on, it's about time we had a chat." He waited for Jon to sit. "I think you're trying to play clever games with me." He looked directly at Jon. "You were going to come and report to me twice a day so that I knew you were in school, weren't you?" The stare was still there, unmoving, persistent.

"Well that's what I'm doing, aren't I?"

"You know what I mean. You are supposed to go to lessons too, you know." Jon said nothing. He just listened. Keep quiet and listen. Find out what they know, then they can't catch you out. That's what usually worked.

"Where did you get to?"

"Went to maths and science – you ask the teachers."

"I have." The stare returned. "Come on, where have you been when you've been out of lessons?"

"Dunno." Why – he didn't know why, but it was always the right thing to say. He couldn't understand that Old Fisher had to get him talking, had to scratch about for any scraps of information on which to base his next report, any bit of information that would help him build up a picture. But he knew what to do and he did it.

"What d'yer mean, 'Dunno'?"

"Dunno 'cos ah dunno." The boy's frustration was scarcely hidden. The teacher noticed. "Well, all I want to know is where you've been. You've not been around the toilets again, I hope – anyway, they're out of bounds during lessons." Jon said nothing.

"You know your mother's due to see me in the morning, with you as well." Again, there was the stare. "Jon, I'm trying to talk to you, trying to help you. Don't just sit there with that dumb insolence of yours and tell me … " The boy was on his feet and had lurched away from the man, out of reach and nearer the door. Out of sight in the corridor he breathed again, deeply and quickly, then took off. He ran until he had turned two corners and could no longer hear Old Fisher's noisy ranting.

Next morning his mother jerked angrily at the thin curtains and more light found its way into the room. He lay still for a moment.

"School, come on, we've both gotta go, or had you forgot?"

"What d'yer want ter bother for – be the same old crap as last time." He turned away.

"I said get up, you stupid little sod." She whipped away the bedclothes and Jon leapt to his feet. He faced his mother, and she returned his stare. "This has got to stop. No more pissing about, it's got to stop. You've gotta go to school."

"School's crap. I hate the bloody place and it's piss-all use."

"You've got to go to school. It's the bloody law. I couldn't give a shit what you do there so long as you bloody go." Jon was struggling into his clothes, cursing as he did so. "And you're goin'! I ain't being pissed about like this again."

The boy turned so that his face was a couple of feet from his mother's. "For fuck's sake, can't you bloody leave off? I hate the fuckin' school, I hate the fuckin' teachers and I fuckin' hate … "

The blow caught the side of his face. It knocked him slightly off balance. He recovered enough to glare at the woman in front of him. He raised his arm, then seized a small chair which he smashed down in front of her. He glared at her again then turned towards the door. She followed him downstairs and ten minutes later they left the house.

It was the first time that mother and son had been anywhere together since the second visit to the hospital. Jon thought she might have been seeing something of the man he had met in the house a week or so before, but he didn't really care. Other kids stared as they arrived at school and Jon seethed with anger and embarrassment. Getting the whole stupid business over and done with seemed the best thing. And he was right. If only he could have known that.

He could not bring himself to sit down next to his mother outside Old Fisher's room. There was little room to stand out of the way and the corridor was a busy one. Several kids waited to see what was going on, then Tracey arrived with her little gang.

"Hi Jon. Toy-boy again? Miss Lambert won't like it!" Jon ignored her and eventually the girls moved on down the corridor. Then Jon wanted to pursue them, to strike them from behind and hurt them so they would leave him alone in future. Instead his rage turned back in on himself and he visibly shrank up against the wall.

"Soddin' cheek! Who's she think she is?"

"Dunno." Jon started off towards the toilets.

"Now where d'yer think you're going?"

"Toilet, where d'yer think?"

For once he found peace there. The caretaker had visited the toilets earlier that morning and the windows were still open. A few early customers arrived and went, none of whom he knew. There was the comfort of a warm radiator and he leant against it for a few moments and let his rage evaporate. When the school had quietened he emerged and returned to Mr. Fisher's office. His mother had gone. For a moment hope soared and he imagined her shouting at Old Fisher then storming out of the school. He was sorry to have missed that. But then the teacher looked out of his office into the corridor.

"Where have you been, Jon? You're keeping us waiting." Jon approached slowly and Old Fisher stood to one side to let him in. "Just sit over there, will you?" Jon sat near his mother, head down; ignoring her and staring hard at the floor.

"Now then, I've already explained your situation to your mother. She understands that the education authorities will prosecute her if you don't come to school regularly. That means she could be fined. Did you realise that?"

"Course 'e does. 'E knows exactly what'll 'appen. I'm always on at 'im about it. 'E just won't do what 'e's told." She paused for a moment. For a moment she had the man's sympathy, but not the boy's. None of this made sense to Jon. Why couldn't she get on with it and then go? For once, he almost wanted to go along to class.

"I don't know why you can't do anything with him like, you know, punish 'im." His mother was staring straight at the teacher, unflinching. Old Fisher looked back wearily and gathered some papers. He tapped the bundle onto the table as if gathering his thoughts.

"Do you remember Year 8 – when we tried to keep Jon behind for a detention?" The man watched for some sort of acknowledgement. "When we finally caught up with him and made him wait behind, you complained." Again he waited, wondering whether the woman would respond. She did not. "It was not very helpful."

"Yeah, well, we was goin' out like, like I said at the time."

The teacher sighed then turned to Jon. "You'll have your GCSEs next year. You should be halfway through the course by now, but you've got an awful lot of catching up to do."

There was another pause, then the woman picked up her plastic bag from the side of the chair where she had left it. She held it on her lap and glared back at the man. "So you're doin' sod all. Right? But you want me to control 'im and if that don't work, you're gonna take me to court!" She was furious again. Jon could still feel her hand on his face.

"Mrs. Quinn, the law says that your responsibility is to get him to school. If he does not arrive at school, we are obliged to report the matter to the authorities. They decide what to do then." She was starting to get up again but Old Fisher wanted to finish what he was saying. "If you get Jon to come to school, or bring him to school, and then he leaves before the end of the day, then he is responsible. This too can be reported. Then, if it goes to court, the concern is to make Jon do what we both want – to be in school, getting some work done."

Nothing new had been said. What could change?

Jon understood; the adults had said what they always said. His mother couldn't make him come to school and she wasn't really bothered anyway. Why Old Fisher said he wanted him at school, he couldn't imagine – no one there liked him. The school could do nothing for him, so why should he let the bastards touch his life? His new-found resolution came to his aid again. He knew they saw him as a complete waste of space; trouble followed him into their school and he would leave next year anyway.

His mother looked across at him. For a second, the memory of some sort of fondness lingered but anger gripped her now. Jon was such a bloody wind-up merchant. Still, he'd probably bugger off soon. Perhaps she'd get her life organised with this new bloke. She looked up at the clock – time she was off.

"Like I said, I do me best. It's up to 'im now."

Jon was already standing up. He had had enough of school for the day.

His mother picked up her bag. "And I'm not paid for me work 'ere." She too was on her feet.

"Well, thank you for coming." Old Fisher was gathering up some papers with his back to the door. Jon left before his mother and was out of sight when the teacher turned around again.

"Where's Jonathan, Mrs. Quinn?"

"Gone to class, ain't 'e? That's what you wanted, innit?"

****

"Morning, Jonathan – good to see you." The teacher paused. "Is there any particular reason why you're late?"

"Bin with Mr. Fisher."

"Well, just sit yourself down." Jon hesitated. "No book?" He shook his head. "You'll have to share with someone." The teacher looked around the class. "Sit over there with Michael, he's brought his book this morning. Just move up a bit please, Michael and make room for Jonathan." There was no response. "Come on Michael, just help out a bit please." The boy now moved himself and his books right away from the desk that the teacher had indicated to Jon.

Jon sat alone in the nearest desk.

"Jonathan, you can't sit over there by yourself – you'll have to share with someone." But she didn't say who; the class watched and the time ticked by.

"He can sit with me, Miss," Tracey called out from her corner of the room. The other girls grinned at Jon. "Shove up, you stupid cow, make room for 'im." Tracey pushed her friend so hard that she had to grab hold of her desk. The legs of her chair scraped across the floor.

"Look what you're doing!" Both girls were laughing now. For a moment school was fun.

"Come on Jonathan, sit over there with Tracey, please." Jon remained where he was, rooted to his chair. "Well, if you're just going to stay there, I'll have to give you extra work at the end of the lesson."

"It's all right, Miss." Tracey quickly made her way over to Jon and sat down. There was a chorus of oohs and aahs. Jon turned his head away and, slowly, the lesson began.

The desks were good like that – they sloped towards you and that made it easier to get comfortable. Once you were settled, you could turn your face towards the front of the class and the upward projection of the desk lid would keep you looking attentive and interested. He ignored Tracey.

His eyelids drooped for a few moments, then he heard Mrs. Lambert's warm-up question. "Come on now Jonathan, pay attention and remind us where we finished last time." There was a pause. "Oh, of course, you weren't with us, were you? Susie, do you remember?" The girl struggled with some words and Jon left them to get on with it.

He was still there at the end. Before the bell rang, the noise of the others starting to pack up roused him. He lifted his head from the desk, blinked and looked around. For twenty minutes the lesson had gone on around him and he had remained unscathed, untouched. He was unmarked, unaffected by the process. For a moment he watched the other kids.

One of the girls stood in front of the teacher. For a moment Jon's urge to leave was suspended as he watched her argue about homework. From outside someone pushed open the door, then continued along the corridor. Only Jon noticed and he quietly left the room. Outside he decided to go and see Old Fisher, just to tell him that he'd managed to stay for a whole lesson. As he moved off the bell rang.

The next morning Jon had almost reached school when he remembered that he had no books again; he recalled the invitation to sit and share with the girls. Nearby was the place where kids sometimes left bikes but there were none there this morning. There was no hurry and for a moment he looked around more carefully to see whether anything else of interest had been left there. The exhilaration of his ride down to the café came back to him and he remembered sweeping people out of the way as the bike had propelled him down through the town. He swore, turned his back on school then set off on foot.

Towards the centre of the town he was distracted for a while by other kids of his age hanging around the edge of the market. He thought he recognised one or two and moved on. At the other end of the market was the pub, dark and shut up at this time of day. Two old men sat on one of the benches outside, soaking up the early morning sun. They reminded him of Steve and Barry, or Paul and Old Jimmy; now he had a way into their conversations, a sort of passport. He knew that he could have gone over to these two men outside The Railway and joined in on some pretext, had he wanted to. But he had no need. His stomach spoke and soon he found himself outside Jimmy's café.

Jimmy quickly noticed him and came back outside with a plate of eggs and chips. Why the old man treated him like this Jon didn't know.

Soon Paul came over from the garage. "Oh, it's you again, is it?

You must like Old Jimmy's grub then." He grinned, looking towards the old man. "Not bad, is it?"

"Dunno."

"What d'yer mean, 'Dunno?' You come here scoffing this grub and you don't know whether it's any good?" Fortunately Jon looked up at this point. He had sensed the different tone in the man's voice and now he saw the laughter in his eyes. He made an effort to smile back even though he felt uncomfortable.

The old man stood up, plate in hand. "I'll 'ave to give 'im a job next time, washing up."

Paul remained there for a few moments. "Now then, are you just 'angin' about again or do you want to earn a few bob?"

"Whad'yer mean?" Jon stopped chewing for a moment.

"I ain't offerin' you a job, but I've got some odds and ends to do. Keep you busy for the rest of the day. Wanna earn yerself some money, twenty quid maybe?"

Jon was not expecting this. Why he had come back to the café he did not know, but here he was. "Yeah, I reckon so – give it a try." They stood up and Jimmy watched them cross over to the garage.

Chapter Eleven

The girl on the calendar smiled a welcome as Jon stepped into the darkness of the workshop. The late morning sun slanted across her and Paul noticed Jon's interest. "She's probably somebody's great-grandma now." He pointed to the date on the calendar. "Still, lovely pair of tits."

Jon smiled too. This one did not come with noisy friends, did not call after you, did not nag. Again he thought of the girl in the pub doorway.

Paul led the way to a side of the workshop that was littered with scrap, the leftovers from his work – oily rags, cans, a few broken tools and discarded parts. Here and there, scattered over the pile, lay a family of blue boxes that had once sat neatly along a shelf. Now they were casualties to be cleared away. Once they had gone there would be space to park a small car. Around the space there ran a small workbench, lit only by a small window and a filthy light bulb.

Paul started. "I thought …" His voice trailed off. "Look, I need to get this tidied so I can get one or two more cars in. I reckon it'll take the rest of the day to shift and sort it all out." Jon listened, thinking of the twenty pounds. He looked through the outer door, beyond the roadway, where Jimmy was on duty outside his café.

"There's a couple of large oil drums outside, one for metal scrap and the other for rubbish, rags and paper. You'll have to sort it as you go. I'll be around so you can always ask me if you get stuck. What d'yer think?"

"Yeah, I'll have a go." He thought again of the twenty pounds and about school.

"There's some rubber gloves somewhere over there – I'd put them on, if I were you." And that was it. Paul walked over to a car in the main part of the workshop and picked up some tools.

Jon found the gloves and pulled them on. They felt cold at first but he soon forgot this and hauled some large pieces out of the pile. He carried them outside into the bright light and dropped them into an empty oil drum. The bits clattered on top of one another, then came to rest. It was a satisfying sound, a satisfying start, and after a few more journeys he was starting to make an impression on the pile of rubbish.

"How're yer gettin' on, then?" Jon realised that Paul was standing next to him. "Hmmm – looks all right, a good start." Jon felt a moment of pleasure, and relief. "You'll find it bit easier if you just collect small bits to one side, down 'ere perhaps." He indicated a place. "Then carry them out together. Then you'd have fewer journeys to make." Jon said nothing but did as Paul had suggested.

The work was not difficult – Jon had seen older teenagers stacking shelves in the local supermarket, struggling at times with large boxes and crates. He had watched other boys and girls working in a fast-food outlet as their supervisors screamed at them to hurry up and Jon had known that he would not have tolerated such treatment. He picked some more of the blue boxes and took them outside.

Time passed more slowly. At one stage, Paul noticed Jon returning the stare of the girl on the calendar. "Come on mate, she's too old for you." Jon smiled and returned to the pile. Soon one drum was full and Paul showed him how to roll it along to the place where the empties stood. Jon grabbed one of them and started back with it towards the workshop door. Paul followed with another. The pile was definitely looking smaller now and Jon could almost feel the money in his pocket.

Half an hour went by. Jon was not used to being left in peace with a job to do but he was enjoying the movement, the rhythm of his journey back and forth, out into the light and back again into the gloom. For a moment he looked up. The calendar had slid back into the shadows.

"Got a minute, Jon?" Jon stopped and moved towards the other side of the workshop. "Give us a hand with this, will yer?" Paul was struggling to lift the engine out of a small car. It was several inches away from its mountings and was too big for one person to manipulate and lift at the same time.

"Just put that piece of wood under there, will yer?" Paul

indicated the place. "That's it – make sure it's right through, then we'll see what happens." Jon watched the man's face as it contorted with the effort. "Right, now." Something slipped. "Quick, for Christ's sake!"

The wood slid home. Jon stood up straight, still wondering whether he had done the right thing.

"Well done, mate." Jon looked up blankly at the man's quick smile. "Dinner time soon." They shifted another drum, washed their hands and went over to the café.

He couldn't remember eating a proper school lunch. He often heard the other kids talk about school dinners but it suited him better to eat outside the chippy, or anywhere else where other children's food was available. With these other children he was most enterprising, planning where to stand to watch them buy their food, calculating where best to meet someone, how best to avoid someone, but he could not really remember what the food was like after he had wolfed it down.

Jimmy's food was good. Jon sat waiting for the meal, enjoying the smell of hot pies, relishing the sort of appetite that comes after hard work. He just sat, and there it was, a good meal put down in front of him.

They spoke little while they ate. From time to time Jon realised that Jimmy was watching him. He didn't mind.

"Tea, then?"

"Fine."

Paul shoved his plate across the table. "Then we'd better get back."

"Don't let him drive yer too 'ard." Jimmy was picking up their plates and cutlery.

Paul laughed. "No chance of that – he's paid by results, remember?" Jon managed to digest this. He felt very comfortable now, but soon they had drunk their tea and it was time to return to the workshop.

Jon looked around. The pile was still there and the afternoon had begun to drag; ahead of him now was steady work. To one side Paul worked on alone, seemingly unconcerned. Things from beyond the workshop troubled Jon again: school – would he be able to keep Old Fisher off his back? What would his mother do if there was trouble with the law? What about Bill? Would he be able to keep away from him? A large carton stuffed with small items of rubbish disintegrated in his hand halfway between the pile and the door. The remains of the carton slid gently down onto the floor. What the fuck did Steve think he was doing, sending him to this crap job?

He kicked out at some of the bits he had put to one side. Paul, away at the far side of a large car, did not react. Moments later, Jon caught the door frame as he carried out an armful of rags and paper rubbish. The torn boxes, the pieces of plastic and sheets of cardboard spread out across the front of the workshop, enjoying their freedom. They bounced along, letting themselves be carried further by a stiff breeze. He felt their mockery.

"Shit – fucking shit!" He turned away from the mess and slumped down on an old chair near the littered workbench. "Fuckin' rubbish!"

"What's up, mate?"

"Bloody job – I'll never finish!" Jon glared at the floor.

"Fed up? Gotta get used to it. Gotta do the rough jobs first, gotta do what someone'll pay you to do. That's how you get started." Jon scraped his feet on the floor under the chair but made no attempt to get up. The man continued. "The clearing up's gotta come first – there's bugger all else you can do over there." Jon remained still.

"Well, it's up to you. You did real well before dinner. Why give up now?" He continued. "The money's there if you want to finish the job, otherwise you might as well get on yer bike."

Jon had forgotten the bike, but now he reacted. "Shit! Where is the bloody thing?"

"Keep yer 'air on. Old Jimmy's got it safe, round the back of the café."

"Well, sod this crap, I'll never get it finished." The man laughed and watched the boy. "Just give us half the money – half the job's done at least."

"No, mate. The deal is that you do the whole job."

"Just a con then, innit ? Yer get someone started then they get pissed off with it and off they go. Easy, innit? Bloody con."

"I'm not paying out for half a job – and you've had a free lunch." Jon got up from the chair.

"Come back tomorrow and finish it off, if you want. After that, the deal's off."

Jimmy was at the back of the café.

"Where's me fuckin' bike, then?"

"'Ere, what's up then, Jon?"

"I'm off – soddin' crap job. Where's me bike?"

"What d'yer mean, 'crap job'? It got yer a free lunch about an hour ago!"

"Yeah, but it's a con, innit?"

"What d'yer mean, con?"

"It's bleedin' easy, innit?"

"Don't follow."

"'E got me started on a job, then when it gets too much, 'e tells me to piss off. Says I've got to finish the job if I want me money."

"What was the deal 'e offered yer? You move the stuff then 'e pays yer twenty quid?"

"Yeah."

"What are yer moaning 'bout then? All yer gotta do is finish the job and take the money. 'Ow long 'as 'e given yer ter finish?"

"Tomorrer. That's all – bleedin' joker!"

"Well, 'ow long d'yer reckon it'd take yer ter finish, then?"

"Bleedin' hours!"

"'Ow many 'ave yer spent so far?"

"'Bout four."

"And yer more than 'alfway done, ain'tcha?"

"S'pose so."

"Go and finish off, then, and get yer money! All this whingeing – you could've finished by now!"

Jon sat in silence for a moment.

"I'll put a brew on. See if you'll see any sense then."

Jimmy returned with two mugs. Jon had gone and Jimmy wondered whether he had been too direct, too forthright.

Jon was halfway home when he remembered the bike; in his anger he had forgotten it. The afternoon was hot and the long, uphill walk tired him. His mother had not left so much as a penny anywhere in the house but there was some food in the fridge. Jon carried it to the sofa and switched on the television. He was there when his mother returned from work.

The evenings were much lighter now and the warmth of the day lingered on. His mother was preparing to go out again and Jon watched her performance with her make-up. She did not ask about school and Jon left the house before she got the chance. Jon felt a great urge to see Steve, to tell him that the job was crap. He thought of the ten pounds the man owed him. Would Steve help him get a job somewhere else? It was too late to find him at the hospital so Jon set off towards the pub.

The town centre was quiet. The shops and businesses had closed and some litter from the market around the corner blew across the empty pavement. A few early customers were sitting outside. He found Barry with some friends at a corner table. He stopped, uncertain.

"Hiya, Jon! Yer lookin' for Steve?"

"Er, yeah."

"Don't think 'e'll be in tonight – football, in the main park. You'll catch him there all right; 'e's nuts about the game." The others laughed.

"Ta, then." Jon was off again.

"Gotcha, yer little bastard." Jon had run into Bill on the steps of the pub.

"What d'yer want?" Jon realised quickly that the pub entrance was very public, not the best place for Bill's purposes. One or two of the customers looked their way, but walked past.

Before Jon could say any more, Bill rifled his pockets but found them empty. "Where's all this money you're supposed to have got me?"

Jon shook himself free now. "Dunno. I got some today, but the bloke wouldn't 'and it over. I'll 'ave it in a day or two."

"Bollocks!"

The young man easily blocked his way. Then Jon remembered – Bill couldn't run fast. Jon had remained on the top step and now looked down at him. He was angry. Why should this bastard push him around and make his life a misery? Just one shove and he was gone, taking down with him a few chairs and a small table. By the time Bill had got up, Jon had disappeared.

Jon got to the pitch just as the whistle was blown for half-time.

"What yer doing here then, Jon?"

"Couldn't find you in the pub." He was still breathing heavily.

"You in a hurry? Someone chase you here?"

For once, Jon was feeling a little pleased with himself. "Yeah, some miserable git. Thinks 'e's 'ard."

"Wasn't that animal that thumped you the other day, was it?" Steve watched Jon very closely.

"Yeah." Jon paused for a moment and moved uncomfortably. "Won't bother me again." Jon thought of the money and of other possibilities in his life. There was just a chance, no more than a chance, that Bill might give up.

"Been down that garage again?"

"Yeah."

Steve sensed that something was wrong. "Any good?"

"Load a' crap!"

"What does that mean?"

Jon shrugged his shoulders. Steve looked straight at him – his question was not going to go away. "Useless bleedin' job."

"What job?"

"In the garage, clearing up," Jon explained.

One of the players called over to Steve, who moved away. "Gotta go now. See yer after the match."

Despite himself, Jon stayed and watched the game. He really wanted to leave, he wanted to treat this difficulty as he always treated difficulties, by running away. But he was still here, ready to raise his voice against someone who had failed him. He stayed because he was angry with someone on whom he had relied, someone he had decided to trust. Jon had let Steve take over part of his life and Steve had held out the prospect of something better, of escape. Now, as far as Jon was concerned, Steve was answerable. Jon waited for the end of the game.

He stood among a handful of spectators who took no notice of him. They watched a game which burst into life from time to time then died away again. Jon watched the spectators shouting and jeering, like the crowds on television, like the kids at school. He felt safe here where no one heeded him, where he could remain invisible amongst all the noise. No one was bothering him and he could enjoy the game and the anonymity that came with it.

Afterwards he found Steve easily. Steve spoke first: "What did yer think of that little lot?" Jon said nothing. Steve continued, "Not bad for a bunch of cripples", and smiled to himself. Jon was looking away.

"So, what's up with the job, then?"

"No use."

"What d'yer mean – you've only been there five minutes!"

"Yeah, but it's a real drag, just sorting out rubbish."

"Is that all he wants, just sorting out rubbish?"

"Yeah, metal in one place, paper in another, just like a bleedin' dustman."

Steve remembered his team-mates, on their way to the pub. He asked himself why he was bothering with this stupid bloody kid who seemed to be in trouble with just about everybody. Steve felt trapped with him. It was like having a younger brother or sister to take care of – they were a pain, but if you didn't bother, they'd get into trouble. He knew all about avoiding involvement with patients, but he wasn't really involved with this kid – he was just helping him out a bit. For a moment he wondered what it would have been like to have had a brother.

"Let's get a drink. Yer coming?"

Jon shook his head. "No money." Jon looked aside then caught Steve's eye. The older boy smiled and shook his head. "That's all right – didn't bother you before." They set off to follow the others.

Jon was still very unsure of himself with so many of Steve's friends around but the beer was good. He sat back in his chair and looked around. Between glances towards the door of the bar, he tried to catch Steve's attention. He knew that the job business had to be sorted out and he sensed that Steve had more to say.

Steve was caught up in a discussion of the game and picking a team for the next match but he too knew that there was more to be said. They finished their first drinks and there was a lull in the conversation. Someone collected the empties and Steve put some money in the kitty.

"I think you'll have to pay your way next time you come in 'ere, yer know!" For a moment Jon was alarmed but then he heard Steve's gentle laugh. "Jokin'. Anyway – we'll, just 'ave to get this job business sorted."

"What d'yer mean?" Jon was genuinely puzzled. "That's not a job, clearing up rubbish like that. That's just crap." The sour expression was back on his face. He turned away from Steve. "Who wants a shit job like that?"

"What d'you expect? He wants a job done. He offers you money to do it. You say you'll do it, then you get fed up part way through. You don't want to finish it. What bloody use are you?"

Chapter Twelve

The counter-attack hurt Jon. Steve's words had got under his skin and it disturbed him that he did not want to run away, that he was waiting to take more grief. He sensed that he had to reply. Not to reply would simply mean more questions, and Steve was waiting.

"It's bleedin' borin'." The phase was a cop-out really, but it meant that he could continue to whine and complain; the phrase established a grouse, provided a pretext, an excuse for continued resentment. He could keep on blaming someone else.

"So what?" Steve was very annoyed. He was no longer looking at Jon, but stared hard past the boy towards the bar. For the first time, Jon saw the tension in his fingers, saw them tap sharply against the table-top. He had used another trigger, another provocation, another phrase that kids like to use and Steve had turned it back against him. Jon watched Steve take a long pull at his drink and waited until he had put down the glass again. He was not sure which way the conversation would go so remained quiet.

"D'yer think you're gonna find another job, just like that?" Steve continued. "What if you get another job? What if it gets boring? Run away again, I suppose?" Steve looked straight at Jon. "Remember, you can't go to any big employer – that Paul bloke's just right; the old boy at the café'd be all right too. No office, no paperwork and cash out of the till."

For a moment Jon thought of the money he'd seen in Jimmy's till. He'd only got a quick glance, but it had been enough for him to take notice. Jon was trying to make sense of what Steve was saying. It began to dawn on him that he was very exposed, like a small creature caught out in the open, like a wild hamster. He ran for cover, where he would feel safe, where this friend could not follow. He shot down a small hole and turned round sharply. "Nah, stick it. Don't want no more of that crap. Fucked if I'm going back there."

While Jon was still outside his small hole, Steve could reach him, but now he had run for it the chance had gone. They glared at each other across the table.

"You're mad, even more bloody stupid than I thought you were!" Steve put down his glass again. "All jobs have boring bits. Mine does. But you keep going, show them what you're made of, move onto something better." Steve drank again while Jon watched him closely, suspiciously.

"Anyway, someone has to do the boring bits, so you get on with them, get the boring bits out of the way. Then there's a chance that something more interesting will come up."

Jon shook his head and looked away. "Nah, they're all the same, them bosses. Just like where me mum works. Bastards want to wear you out."

Steve looked towards his friends from the football club, further along the table. "Well, it's your bloody look-out." He allowed himself to finish the rest of the beer. "Don't tell me, you're back to school in the morning."

Some of Steve's friends looked their way.

Jon got up. "See yer," he said, and was gone.

"Where the 'ell a' you bin all day?" She had heard him come in and was standing, ready for him, in the hall. Somewhere behind her was the noise of the television.

"I just saw some mates on the way home. Stopped out with ... " He tried to get past but she stood there in front of him.

"That bleedin' Fisher was on the phone again. Caught me at bleedin' work, an' all." She looked hard at him. "Yeah, you know what I'm on about. You ain't bin near the place all day, you stupid little sod! 'E's getting onto the council about you. Said 'e 'ad to."

As she spoke, the man who had been there before came out of the living room. He leant against the wall, just behind her.

"Just let me go up to me room, will yer?" There was something of a plea in the boy's words but his mother ignored them.

"Not till we've sorted this lot out, you're not going nowhere." Neither adult moved.

"I just wanna get something, that's all." Again he was ignored. His mother sensed the man behind her and stood her ground.

She recalled the betrayals, the sense of emptiness and total uncertainty that hung over her whenever men had intruded in her life before. It was impossible not to. For years coping alone had nearly finished her but now, with this Dave, there was the flicker of life within her again. Now her son found her unyielding.

She had had enough of this little toe-rag and he was not going to spoil things for them. She was going to have to put her foot down. Too late, perhaps years too late – it didn't really matter, she was going to try. For too long he had made her life impossible – without him things would have worked out. It was time to think of herself and this bloke, Dave. Yeah, feeling sorry for the boy was one thing, but she wasn't going to let him balls up her future.

Jon took the only way out, the front door.

He had never stayed out all night before and he was still hungry. The bins behind the chippy provided some scraps – they were still warm; the shop had closed just before he arrived hoping to scrounge something more substantial. Then he moved off slowly to the open space. Jon huddled himself in a corner, overlooking the burnt-out car. Although it was not a cold night, he shivered in his shirtsleeves.

He had not been there long when three boys of about his age came along. One of them was carrying a white plastic bag. Had there been only two of them he might have sought their company. He watched as they took out another bag, poured some glue into it then took it in turns to hold the mouth of the bag over their noses and breathe in deeply.

When they had gone he went over to the old car and picked up the discarded bags. There was enough glue left for his purposes. Someone had thrown some old curtains into the back of the car and they covered the seat springs that had been exposed by the fire. He sniffed at the bags for a while then settled himself amongst the filth and mess in the back of the car.

He went back home just as other kids were going to school. The house was locked and there was no response to his angry knocking; his mother must have gone into work. He remembered the window that his mother sometimes forgot to shut. Round at the back, he struggled with the lean-to and the down-pipe, reached down through the fanlight and opened the main window. Inside he found some food. He felt better and a little confidence returned. He slumped onto the sofa and considered how to handle the school business. Soon, he was asleep. Two hours later, he was woken by a persistent knocking at the front door.

Jon heaved himself up to the window and stood behind the tatty curtains. For a moment he could see no one there. Then he looked down again and saw Old Butty, all four-foot ten of her. She raised the knocker once more, then waited. Did she know that he was there? She turned around, giving the whole of the street the benefit of a slow inspection. It was clearly to her liking so she addressed the front door again. This was where her business lay. If he didn't open the door, she'd be there all bloody day.

"You took yer time. I thought you should be at school. Is yer mum in?"

"No. What d'yer want?"

"You ain't seen anyone hanging about, 'ave yer? Them people over the road said they saw someone 'anging about earlier this morning, after yer mum 'ad gone out."

"Nah, I ain't seen anyone." This was not good enough for Old Butty.

"Shouldn't you be in school? I know you ain't old enough to leave."

"Ain't feeling too good today." A glimmer of truth showed on the boy's face. The old woman noticed.

"Well, just tell yer mum what I told yer, will yer?" With that she was gone.

He thought about lunch – it was getting on for midday so he set off. His journey to school yielded half a bag of chips and a surprisingly large piece of fish, as well as two pound coins from a minor victim he caught unawares. Old Fisher was in the playground. Here, away from his office, he seemed more approachable. Without realising it, Jon had chosen a good time to speak to him.

"Hello, Sir."

"Hello Jon. Just arrived?"

"Been ill, Sir. Felt a bit better after dinner, so here I am."

"Okay, but make sure you bring a note tomorrow." With that the teacher returned to his office and the grubby coffee mug.

Jon did try hard that afternoon. For once he really wanted to be able to approach Old Fisher after school to show him that he was still there, in school. At first he resisted the temptation to skip a lesson, maths with yet another stand-in teacher, but before three o'clock, he was standing outside the back entrance, unsure of his next move. The money in his pocket was a comfort but he knew that it would soon be gone and he thought of the money Paul owed him. He could walk down to the garage and have another go at getting the tenner he'd earned. Then he thought of the walk back.

Suddenly he remembered that his bike was hidden behind Jimmy's café, and set off.

"'Ello, sunshine. 'Ow are you then?"

"All right. Where's me bike?"

"Friendly today."

"Gotta see Paul, ain't I?"

"You ain't still on about that money, are yer?"

"'E fuckin' owes me!"

"Hmmm." The old man looked straight at Jon. "Could you use a cuppa?" Jon sat down and waited while Jimmy fetched three mugs.

Paul came out of the garage and walked over. "'Ow are yer, Jon?" Jon was wary but he listened. "I really wanted that space cleared." He looked very directly at Jon and studied his face. "D'yer want to finish it off, earn that twenty quid?" Jon had not seen things quite like this; he'd just gone there for his bike. "You'll be all right with some of Old Jimmy's tea inside yer. You've got most of it done already."

The boy sat there for a few moments while the two men drank their tea. Somehow they watched him without looking at him. He knew they were watching, but he could not have put the idea into words however hard he tried. He knew though, knew that he did not have to worry for the moment. He knew that it did not matter whether they really liked him, whether they trusted him – he could get up and go any time he liked, or else he could stay. He did wonder, though, why they had not got on to him about walking out.

"'Nother cup?" He hadn't realised that he had emptied the mug. Jimmy re-filled it and returned with a sausage roll. "Why don't you go and help our mate out? Poor old bugger can't manage on his own."

It was not difficult to follow Paul back to the garage, not difficult to carry on where he had left off. Soon the pile of rubbish was much reduced in size and a sense of purpose began to return.

By seven o'clock the pile had gone and Jon had two tenners in his pocket. He had been clumsy with a broom to start with, but now the grimy, black concrete was clear and the space under the workbench was uncluttered. The tidy rows of small boxes on the shelves above pleased him a little and the girl on the calendar smiled her approval.

When Jon had finished, Paul lifted a small box of tools onto the bench. "If you want to earn any more 'ere, you'll 'ave to learn to use these. I've got some simple jobs that want doing on this Mini." He waved at the old car that was waiting on one side. "If you're smart, I can show you what to do as we go along – if you're smart." He looked at Jon for a moment and raised his eyebrows to emphasise the hint. "Yesterday, with that engine, I could see you'd got the makings. Two quid an hour and I'll give yer a bit more if you're any good. School's no good for yer, that's for sure." He stood there with a spanner in his hand.

Jon looked away.

"I know you ain't really old enough and you won't always be able to get down 'ere just when we want. But if you want to try, you can 'ave a go. You can earn and learn, like." The man watched him again. "What d'yer think, then?"

The boy looked straight back at him and nodded. "Yeah, I'll 'ave a go."

"Come in tomorrer then, soon as yer can get away."

This time Jon cycled home, happy to push against the gradient, thinking about the next day and another twenty quid.

He slowed and turned the bike into the end of his road. Dean stepped out suddenly from behind a post-box and grabbed the handlebars. "'Ello Jon! Where yer bin, mate?"

"Dunno. 'Ere 'n' there."

Dean kept hold of the handlebars. "I was gettin' quite worried about yer. So was our Bill." He let the words sink in. "Billy didn't sound too pleased last time I mentioned you. You upset him or something?"

"Dunno. Don't think so. Why d'yer ask?"

"You'd better 'ave some money on yer, next time he sees yer."

Dean looked fixedly through Jon, as if he could see his older brother on the other side. "You'd better get yerself a job if you can't do any better. Bill's gettin' fed up with waiting."

Jon wrenched the handlebars away from the other boy's grasp, then stood to one side, ready to move away.

"Where d'yer get this bike from?" For a moment Jon shivered inside. He said nothing as Dean cast an eye over it. "Must be worth a few quid."

Jon was ready. "Cousin of mine – doesn't need it for the moment. Come over last week."

"Bit a' luck really. Bill might take it to pay off some of yer debt." He was standing in front of the bike now.

"Can't do that – 'es only lent it to me. If 'e asks for it back I'll have to take it."

"Bloody convenient. One minute yer skint, the next you're pissing about on a decent bike." Jon continued to hold Dean's gaze; he had to keep his attention but he felt him take hold of the handlebars again.

"Who d'yer think yer kiddin'? Anyway, you ain't got no cousin. Where does 'e live? First I've heard of any bleedin' cousin."

"I told yer, 'e lent it ter me. 'E's got a van with 'is job right now, but if 'e loses 'is job, the bike goes back." Jon wrenched the bike back again. "Anyway, ah've got to go now. See yer then." The conversation had gone on long enough.

Dean stood with his mouth wide open. "'Ere, hang about!" He watched Jon turn up the alley between the houses and ride away.

Jon's mother was less impressed. Jon had just lugged the bike into the hallway as she reached the bottom of the stairs. "What's that bloody thing doing 'ere? You can take it straight back outside." She was full of herself again. "Where did it come from in the first place? I suppose you nicked it."

Jon recognised the trick, the sort of question that had once confused him. You didn't know which bit to tackle first, the question or the accusation. If you answered the question, the accusation remained and if you challenged the accusation, the question that had not been answered bounced back at you. And if you didn't answer a question you were guilty, of course.

It was like bullying, like Dean getting on to him, then talking about Bill if he wasn't making progress. You had to think all the time, what were the bastards trying to do? Why were they asking the question, where was it going to lead? It was like Bill thumping him, the second blow landing before you'd got over the first – you just tried to protect yourself from all the blows. Now he knew that certain sorts of things were simply best not said.

"Me mate give it ter me."

"Which one, you lying git?"

"Dean."

"Dean? Who's Dean? Not that scruffy little kid I've seen you with?"

"'Ow would I know?" He shifted the bike so that it would not fall over against the heater. "I'll move it later – don't want ter leave the bloody thing outside." He looked protectively at the bike." We ain't got a lock on the shed any more, 'ave we?"

His mother shrugged her shoulders and moved on. "Anyway, it's out the bloody way before Dave comes round. 'E's bringing a Chinese and a video so you can go out if yer like. Take this bloody thing with yer!"

"All right, all right." Jon turned towards the stairs. His mother had not moved.

"Move that bloody piece of crap or Dave will."

"Who does he think he is, then? It's sod all to do with 'im!"

"It's my bleedin' 'ouse and 'e'll move it for me."

"No way. You tell 'im to keep his hands off the bloody thing." Jon stormed up the stairs and his mother heard his bedroom door slam.

Later, he remembered someone undoing quick-release wheels. This was just as well for there were no tools in this house, nothing handy for useful jobs. A few minutes later, he came back down to the bike, removed the front wheel and took the wheel and the bike frame up to his room. Next morning he reassembled it and reached the garage just before ten. He propped the bike out of sight at the back of the workshop and walked over to Paul.

"Ready to start, then?" Paul walked over to the area Jon had cleared the day before. The old Mini stood there, waiting patiently. "Got to get this going. An old customer's had it in her garage for years and she wants to get rid of it."

"Why don't she just flog the thing?"

"Worth bugger-all as it is. If she can sell it as a runner, you know, with an MOT certificate, she'll get a lot more for it."

"And we get the job of putting it straight?"

"Yep. So, you can start by getting these spark plugs out. Use this spanner." He handed Jon a socket-spanner. "Put it on dead straight, then turn it carefully until you can unscrew it completely." He watched as Jon got started. "That's it, not too hard and keep it straight. If it slips, you catch your knuckles …. Right, now you've three more to do. Tell me when you've finished." Paul returned to another car.

Jon had virtually no memory of using tools except when he wanted to smash or break something open but now he enjoyed the sense of control they gave him over these mechanical parts, a sense of power over things that would not move. The first two plugs came out with little trouble.

Then the last plug proved reluctant to turn. With his growing confidence, Jon strained to make it shift. He forgot to keep the spanner straight and the ceramic top of the plug shattered as the spanner slipped suddenly and the back of his hand smacked against the underside of the bonnet. "Fuckin' 'ell – ooh, that bleedin' hurt!"

Paul looked up. "You all right?" Jon had dropped the spanner down past the engine and was gripping his hand.

Paul came over, glanced at Jon's hand and then examined the broken plug top. "See what I mean – hurts a bit, don't it? You'll soon learn to watch out for that."

Jon simply stood there waiting for the reprimand, the bollocking. The man continued, "If you were putting in a new plug it would be different; these old ones are useless now, so don't worry." And that was it. Paul glanced again at Jon's hand and returned to his own work.

Jon set about finding the spanner. "Try looking under the car and round the engine." Jon was on his knees, his arm extended under the car. Eventually, he found the spanner and removed the last plug. Paul came over to join him and worked on the more complicated things such as the carburettor, and Jon found himself learning how to remove wheels and brake drums. Each time Jon finished one of these chores, Paul explained what he was dealing with before starting him on the next job. Sometimes Jon worked on the larger car and quietly, unobtrusively, Paul's ran his eye over each job before explaining the next one.

Later, Jon looked again around the workshop and his pile of rubbish. This time it was clean rubbish, boxes from which he had removed new parts. It was new rubbish, rubbish with a purpose, rubbish which showed that something had been done. Jon was pleased with this pile; it reflected his efforts. The more work he did, the more it grew. It was his to control.

While the men continued their conversation Jon gathered up an armful of small cardboard packages and took them out to the bin where he had spent so much time the day before. As he returned, he came face to face with Jimmy in the doorway. The old man nodded as they passed one another.

"See yer at dinner time."

When Jimmy brought the plates over to their table, he stood for a moment and looked around at his customers. Jon could see two women working out in the kitchen.

"What yer gonna do about school then, Jon?" Jon had forgotten about school for a moment and the question made him pause.

"Dunno, just don't know." Jon shrugged his shoulders. "Sort something out tomorrer. Dunno what, though."

"Lot a silly buggers – you shouldn't be worryin' him about school." Paul turned to Jon. "You can go down the tech when you want a bit o' training. They're a good lot down there."

"'Ang about." Jimmy was bothered. "'E's supposed to go to school. It's all right you givin' 'im a bit a work now and again, like, but they're gonna be after 'im if 'e ain't careful."

Paul shook his head. "What – d'yer think they're gonna come down 'ere lookin' for 'im? No bloody chance!"

"What do yer think they 'ave those truancy officers for – chasing up bloody kids what don't go to school? If they come round 'is 'ome, 'is old lady's not going to be too pleased, is she?"

"Well, 'e'll 'ave ter play it a bit clever, let them think he'll turn up fairly regular then they won't bother 'im." Paul continued with his meal. Jon shoved his plate away across the table and stood up; he had eaten only half what Old Jimmy had put in front of him.

He left the others to talk; discussion over his head always needled him. By the time Paul returned he had finished clearing the rubbish.

"Well done, mate. That's just what I wanted." Paul nodded at the tidy space. Jon was slumped again in the old chair. "Here, what's up now – you're doing all right!"

128

"Fuckin' school – just like them to balls all this up for me. Bastards!"

"What are you going on about? You just got to be careful so they don't find out what you're up to. Just don't tell everyone about yer job. You'll have to go in now and again, just to keep them happy. If yer don't, you'll get into bother. Play the game."

Jon did not move. "Just can't stand the soddin' place, bloody teachers and bloody lick-arse creeps every-soddin'-where."

It was not easy. Another six months and there would be a good chance that they would ignore him – Steve and Barry had been right about that. He remembered older kids who had slowly disappeared from the scene. But until then?

Paul left him and returned to his own work.

"Penny for them, mate." Old Jimmy had come across and was looking him over now.

"What d'yer mean, penny for what?"

"Penny for yer thoughts. What yer thinkin' about now? What's botherin' yer?"

"Bastards at school – don't want them messin' things up, don't want that, do I?"

Paul looked up from an instruction manual. "Don't know how those teachers cope. Buggered if I know how they keep all them bloody kids out of mischief. What would you do with them?" He was looking at Jimmy now. "What would you with them, old man? What would you do with the little sods if they kept on messing about and wouldn't work?" Jon listened to the two men.

Jimmy scratched his head. "Well, if you've got some who'll work – s'pose you've got to keep them busy. Don't know what I'd say to the others. I suppose they're a bit like prisoners of war – got no say in the matter. Can't really blame 'em. Trouble is, they're mixed up together, whether they want to work or not." He looked at Jon. "Well young man, not long to wait; six months and they won't be able to touch you."

Paul shut the manual. "Just try our way Jon – could suit the both of us." He picked up a spanner and a small screwdriver. "Now, what we've gotta do next is this."

Jon was carrying twenty pounds in his pocket when he left for home that night. In the hall he removed the front wheel of his bike so he could carry it back upstairs. He was struggling with the zip on his back pocket, wondering where to hide his money, when his mother came out of the living room towards the kitchen. He turned away instinctively, but she noticed the sharp movement of his hand away from his pocket.

"What the bleeding 'ell 'ave yer got there, you little sneak-thief? Not been after my money again, 'ave yer?"

In the front room, someone moved.

Chapter Thirteen

"I think you'd best let yer mother take care of that." Dave now stood in the living room doorway, close behind Jon's mother.

Jon glared at the intruder. "What the hell do you want?"

The man started towards him but Jon's mother took his arm. "Not now, Dave. Leave the thievin' little sod fer now."

"You let 'im get away with this and you'll never stop 'im." The man made another attempt to get past the woman. This time her efforts had little effect. Jon reached his bedroom door, turned and listened. The bottom stair creaked under the man's weight.

It was still daylight. Jon flung open his bedroom window, climbed down over the outhouse and half jumped, half fell into the back yard. Before he could recover himself a voice screamed from behind, "Just you wait there, you little shit!" The voice came from his own bedroom window, the one he had just abandoned. It was an alien voice and waiting was the last thing on Jon's mind.

"You stupid little bastard – I'll fuckin' sort you out!" The man filled the frame of the bedroom window and Jon noticed him shaking with anger. Jon stood his ground, knowing there was nothing this stupid boyfriend of his mother's could do. The words had been used by his mother dozens of times, but from this other mouth they meant nothing. His mother was welcome to him. The man continued to bellow from Jon's bedroom window.

Jon turned his back on the abuse and stepped into the alley. He looked around and set off to distance himself from his home as quickly as possible. Fifteen minutes later he approached the new-found refuge that was becoming increasingly important to him. Steve was not to be found in the pub but Jon recognised two of his football friends.

"Dunno, mate. Tried his home?"

"Where's that?"

"Somewhere down Lichfield Street, near the station. Hang on." He turned away. "Hey, Simon, where does Steve live? Down Lichfield Street, innit?"

"Yeah, number twenty I think – got a red front door. Can't miss it."

Dean was walking along the other side of the road as Jon left. He approached quickly, took Jon by the arm, then followed alongside.

"What the …"

"Bill said I might find yer round 'ere."

"So what?"

"Well, e's seen yer in the pub. Yer must 'ave some of that money 'e's waiting for."

"Dunno what 'e's talkin' about. Me mate buys me a drink sometimes. That's all. Got no money for bleedin' pubs."

"Just like you ain't got no money for bleedin' bikes, you lying little shit."

"I tell yer, I've no dosh, so piss off, will yer?"

Although Dean no longer frightened him, Jon was still very wary. Even so, he felt a fleeting moment of sympathy for Dean who was even more trapped than he was, caught between his brother and his victims. Yeah, the poor bugger couldn't piss off just like that. He had a job to do.

"Ah don't believe a word, not a bloody word." But Jon was beginning to see through the other boy's casual threats and bluster. His hasty departure from home had meant that his bike was still back in his room. It would have been handy now to help him get away, but then the less Dean saw of it, the better. Would Dave bother with it? He didn't know; all he knew was that he didn't want Dean to follow him to Steve's place, and if he returned to the pub, Dean would probably fetch Bill from somewhere.

Dean could not have walked any closer to Jon. Jon was angry now, angry enough to hit him, to knock down this ridiculous go-between. Fear of him was being pushed out by anger, and Jon felt that he could easily stop Dean physically from following him, but hitting Dean would give Bill another excuse.

There was a little light left in the sky and it was dry. Dean was keeping pace with him as they approached the station. "Where are you off to now?"

"Just walkin'. Where are you going?"

"You owe me, Jon. You've got money, I bloody know you 'ave."
Dean's anger and frustration glared at him. "Don't be so stupid, just
hand it over."

They walked on, like two best mates. Two smaller boys gave
them a wide berth. In the station forecourt there was a vending
machine. Dean inserted a coin. "You ought to be buying this, yer
know."

"I'm going for a piss."

Jon turned into the toilet a few yards along the pathway. As he
looked towards the cubicles he noticed a door that led out another
way. He sprinted along the empty platform, away from the main
part of the buildings, for he knew that Dean would follow very
quickly. Beyond the tracks was a low wire fence. Twice he stumbled
as he scrambled across the rails but then he was beyond the fence
and behind a hedge. He crouched there and listened.

"Jon – where are yer?" He listened as Dean's shouts echoed along
the empty station. "I'll get yer, you stupid bastard!" The station
remained silent at first, then gradually, in the dark space that
divided them, the rails came to life. Hidden away, safe for the
moment in a gap under the hedge, Jon heard a distant rumble.
Slowly a giant hand was pulling an iron curtain between them. The
long lines of steel began to murmur to one another, then the boys
were separated by the deafening rattle and roar of a long train.

Jon waited for a few minutes, then peeped out cautiously. There
was no sign of Dean and Jon wondered what version of events
Dean would give his brother.

It was easy enough to find Steve's home. For a while, Jon stood
on the other side of the road. There was a light on in the front room
and he could see three people watching television. One of them was
Steve. An elderly couple walked by on the pavement, dragged along
by an enthusiastic corgi. The dog greeted Jon in its cheery, doggy
way, but its minders merely glared. When they had gone he felt
uncomfortable and started to look about, concerned that someone
else would notice him there.

Steve's father opened the door.

"Er, is, er Steve about?"

"Sure. Step inside a minute." The man was a bigger, older version
of Steve; he even had the same smile. He held the door open and
moved to one side. Without looking around, Jon entered the hall.

"I'll just fetch 'im. Won't keep yer a moment." The sound of a door clicking open reached Jon.

"Mate a' yours, Steve."

"Who is it?"

"Dunno. Not one of yer regulars. Fetch 'im through, if yer like."

"Hi." Steve was surprised to see him. "You all right?" Steve could see the concern on Jon's face but Jon said nothing. He was relieved to see Steve but, in a house with strangers around, he could say nothing to explain himself.

"You got bother at 'ome?" Jon nodded. "Yer mother?" Jon nodded again. "Let's go out the back for a minute." Steve turned and spoke to his parents in the front room. "We'll be out the back. I'll finish supper in a minute."

Outside they sat on a couple of seats by a plastic table. For a moment Steve left his visitor to sit in silence. He watched Jon drop his chin onto his chest and slouch back in the chair; his wariness had left him now and he felt relaxed enough to ignore Steve.

"Now then, what's up?"

There was no rush, no hurry. Jon's attention returned slowly but, at first, he could not look up at his friend. Steve watched him, still as death; only the rise and fall of his breathing betrayed the life in him. Then, at last, Jon found some words. "Every bastard's on me back. Dean keeps following me about, worrying me about that sodding brother of his."

"That the git who thumped you?"

"Yeah. Can't get him off me back. Then me mother spotted me money when I got home and her new bloke tried to make me hand it over. And Dean's got his thievin' eye on me bike, so I can't leave that anywhere, and the old woman goes spare 'cos I keep it in me bedroom – where else can ah keep the soddin' thing?"

"How did you get away from this bloke?"

"Out the winder."

There was a lot to digest and Steve could sense Jon's desperation.

"'Ow's the job going?"

"All right, I s'pose. How should I know?"

"But you got paid?"

"Oh yeah. No bother."

They sat again in silence, then Steve's mother put her head out of the back door. "Cuppa tea?"

134

"In a minute, Mum. We'll be in in a minute."

"Righto." She spoke to her son but she was looking at Jon. He was staring down at the table, but could feel her gaze. "I'll make a fresh pot later."

"Why does this bloke want your mother to have your money? Have you been borrowing from her?"

"Er, sort of."

"You owe somebody, then?"

"Well, I was skint and I 'ad this other bastard on me back so I er … "

"You nicked money from yer mother?" There was another pause. "You could offer to pay it off, a bit at a time, now you seem to be earning a bit. Get her off yer back."

"But I can't stand 'im, not interfering, like."

"Yeah, but if yer mum gets some of her money back, he'll have no reason to interfere. Anyway, if he does it again, you tell your mum that you'll report him for threatening you. Don't have to go to social services – just tell Old Fisher at school. If he gets on to her about it, she won't like it but it'll put the wind up her."

Jon thought about this for a moment. "What about this other bastard?"

"You mean Dean's brother, whatsisname?"

"Bill."

"You know what the trouble is – it's quite simple really. They think you've got money and they think they can get it off you."

There was another pause. The back door opened and Steve's mother appeared with a tray. "Thought you said only a minute." Jon did not know what to make of her quiet smile. "Some minute that was. You'll need a cup, with all this talking you're doing."

"Thanks Mum." She put the cups and a pot of sugar onto the table and went back inside.

"Did you borrow money from them? Do you owe them money?"

"No. Just money I 'ad to get off other kids."

Steve took up a cup in one hand. "Have you got any money off other kids?"

"A few quid."

"What happened to it? Did you hand it over?"

"Yeah." Jon tried to grip the tiny cup handle, gave up and lifted the cup in both hands.

"All of it?"

"Course I did. Didn't want that bastard after me."

"Trouble is, now he's got some money off you, 'e'll keep coming back for more."

"Yeah, but what can I do?"

"Don't give 'im a bloody thing. Keep away from him and Dean. Now I know, he won't bother you round the pub. He won't bother if he sees there's nothing in it for him. Whatever you do, don't let them find out about your job. Let him forget about you for a while." Steve drained his cup. "And another thing, get yourself a post office account for your money. Don't want that lying about to get nicked."

"What d'yer mean?"

"If you keep you money on you, or somewhere in the house, you're gonna lose it, aren't yer? Your old woman's after it, so's Billy the Bastard."

"But how can I get hold of it once it's in the post office?"

"Just go back and get it out. Don't have to go back to the same place – go to any post office. All you'll need is your pass book."

"What's that?"

"It's a book where they keep a record of what you've got saved. It's like your ID. You'll 'ave to keep it safe somewhere." There was another pause, then Steve stood up. "Fancy some supper?" Jon followed him into the living room.

"This is Jon."

"'Ow do." Steve's father picked up the remote and the sound from the television was suddenly gone. "Sit y'self down, Jon."

Jon smiled nervously then sank into an elderly armchair. It almost swallowed him. From somewhere Steve's mother reappeared. "Steve's supper's ready. Would you like some?"

"Yeah. Er, please." He watched the figures on the television screen. Steve's mother left the room.

"D'yer live round here, like?" Steve's father was looking across at him.

"Nah, other side of town."

"Football is it, then?"

Jon paused then looked at Steve. "Sort of – I watched 'em play the other night."

"Oh, right."

A game started on the television. Steve reached out and turned up the volume. Father and son sat absorbed while Jon watched perfunctorily. During pauses in the commentary he turned his attention to the room. He could have been planning one of his burglaries; he noted the new video recorder and the more expensive-looking ornaments – knick-knacks they were, really. Up on a shelf were some pots that might have had money stuffed in them. Outside he had weighed up the alleyway and the spaces between the larger, semi-detached houses at the back. It was automatic, something you always did. When he had sat outside with Steve he'd noticed there was no lean-to or extension to climb onto. He was aware, he just sensed these things: differences in the buildings, differences in the contents and differences in the people.

Then he found himself wondering where he was going next. What would he find when he got home? He didn't want to face his mother until morning. Here he was warm and comfortable and he could watch the football with the others if it suited – and he could smell something good in the kitchen. Someone was taking a penalty and the commentator's voice called for his attention. Then another, more welcome, voice distracted him.

"Here you are, boys. There's some more outside if you're still hungry. I'll just get the tea." Steve's mother had come back with a tray and four cups and saucers, and still with that warm smile. Jon allowed himself to feel more comfortable and sat with a large plate on his lap. The pizza was good.

"That all right, Jon?" Steve's mother had noticed him eating eagerly.

"Yeah, er thanks."

"What's the score then, boys?" Steve and his dad didn't hear. She looked round at Jon. "Bet you don't ignore your mum like that." Her smile embarrassed Jon now, but he didn't mind too much. It was a kind smile. She turned to the others. "Now then, you two. I bet neither of you know the score."

"One–nil." They spoke in unison and continued to ignore her.

"Did you see that? They are rude, yer know. I bet you're not rude like that." Jon could not smile back and again he felt her curiosity. "So, what d'yer think of his team?"

"Oh, they're all right."

"To hear him talk you'd think they were in the Premier Division. Some hope! At least it keeps 'im out of bother." Jon smiled weakly and tried to watch the television. "I'll leave you all to it, I think."

The three of them said little until the end of the game when the television was switched off and Jon's unease returned. Steve's mother came back into the room and sat herself at the table. Before she could restart the conversation Jon was getting to his feet. "Gotta go now – school tomorrow." He tried to remember the other words. "Thanks for the supper." Steve showed him to the door and stepped outside with him.

"Just remember, keep right away from them two and turn up at school as often as you can. Come down the pub next Monday – let me know how you're doing."

"Yeah. Cheers mate. See yer." Jon walked off into the warm streets.

He had not given a lot of thought to where he might spend the night. The supper and the company of these people had lessened his wariness and he thought it would be worth taking a look back home. Dave's threats were less immediate now.

There was a light on upstairs when he got there. The front door was locked and he realised that he had forgotten his keys in the rush to leave the house. He remembered his own bedroom window, which had provided an escape route. He walked back down the front path then noticed a strange car parked outside. A street light revealed his bike in the back. He tried the car doors but they were all locked. For a moment he fumed. Around at the back of the house he could see that his bedroom window gaped open. With the help of a dustbin he scrambled up onto the outhouse roof. For a moment his feet scraped noisily on the rough tiles and he stopped to listen for sounds from inside. A final effort and he clambered back into his room. The door onto the landing was shut.

There was enough light for him to see across his room. He paused, listening very intently, ready to fling himself back out through the window if necessary. There was nothing. Slowly he moved again. From the wardrobe he took out a screwdriver and a piece of stiff wire, an old coat hanger. He moved confidently downstairs and out through the front door.

From the street he could see that the light had been turned out in his mother's room. He worked on the far side of the car and soon had the door open. He made only one grating noise and paused for a moment, looking up anxiously at the window. There was no sign of life.

Five minutes later, he was back in his room. He put his bike to one side and half-closed the window. As best as he could, he wedged the door with a chair then, without undressing, got into bed.

It was the rattling of his bedroom door that woke Jon. It was still dark and he sat up, confused, trying to escape the clutches of a deep sleep. Outside a man's voice shouted at him to open the door. Jon staggered from his bed and made sure that the chair was still shoved hard up under the door handle. The room resounded with heavy blows, as if some savage beast were trying to get at him. His door shook and tried to tear itself away from its own hinges; there couldn't be much time left before it would collapse. Jon peered round at the window, which was still open.

"Open this door!" It was Dave's voice. "Open up or you'll get a bleedin' good 'iding, you thieving little shite!"

One of the door panels cracked under another blow. Jon listened for a second; there was no sound from his mother and, for a brief moment, he wondered whether she was safe.

"Fuckin' kill you when I get in there!" Another panel cracked but the door still held secure in its frame. Jon wriggled his way out onto the outhouse roof, reached back into his bedroom and dragged his bike after him. For a moment he almost let go and was terrified at the thought of the bike smashing onto the yard below. Together, somehow, the machine and the boy reached the ground. Before he could use it Jon had to fix the front wheel back into the forks so he carried it out of sight, into the alleyway. He expected to hear footsteps running round from the front of the house at any moment, but Dave's voice assailed him still from the window. Jon knew that he was safe.

Jon's sense of alarm made way for anger at the way he had been disturbed. He pushed down hard on the pedals and rode off into the feeble darkness of the early morning.

The station was lit up. Jon bought a cup of coffee and a roll in the cafeteria and sat watching someone unloading newspapers outside. *Maggie Mad at Mark*, cried the headline. Rich bastards! There was a picture of an expensive-looking car somewhere in a rally.

Jon was leaning against the café wall with his bike when Jimmy arrived to open up at half-past six.

Chapter Fourteen

It was one of the best days he had had for a long time. Paul and Jimmy had been surprised by his early arrival but said little. There was plenty to do and Jon still enjoyed learning new skills. Despite his lack of sleep he made an effort to stay alert. After lunch Paul set off to get some parts.

"You'll be all right. Don't suppose anyone'll come, apart from the bloke who left this Ford. Just tell 'im it'll do for the moment but he'll have to bring it back next week. Okay?"

Soon afterwards the Ford's owner turned up.

"Paul about?"

"Nah – gettin' spares."

"Oh. I'm come for me car, the Ford. D'yer know if it's ready?"

"Oh yeah, it's ready. 'E says it'll be all right for the moment, but you'll 'ave ter bring it back next week."

"Right then – got the keys?" Jon fetched them from the workbench at the back of the garage.

The car would not start. Before he got out of the car, the owner released the bonnet, scowling as his stretched forward to find the catch. Jon raised the bonnet and peered underneath. He had helped Paul to work on the car during the morning. "'Ere. I think we've got another one of these." He returned with a new length of cable and inserted it. The car started.

The man looked up at him through the driver's window. "You bin 'ere long, mate?"

"Nah, not really."

"Tell Paul I'll give 'im a bell." He drove off.

Paul soon returned.

"Everything all right?"

"Yeah, 'cept the Ford wouldn't start when the bloke came."

"What 'appened?"

141

"I found another one of them leads, over the back there."

"Start all right then?"

"Oh yeah."

"What did the bloke say?"

"Not a lot really. Didn't seem too bothered once it started."

"That's good. Well done, mate."

Jon could still feel the afterglow of Paul's praise when he set off to walk home. He said nothing about the bike, but simply left it behind where it was safe. He thought about the day's money, stuffed deep in his back pocket. There was no car outside his house, so he walked up the path and tried to open the front door. It swung inwards as soon as he tried to insert the key.

He stepped over a broken chair and into the front room where he found his mother. The wound shocked him. The face was familiar, with all its lines and blotches, the same face that usually snarled and screamed and hurled abuse. But now from the corners of the eyes ran tears, still wet. He noticed the torn sleeve and the broken things on the floor. She was very still.

Jon stood and looked at her and wondered what he was going to do.

Slowly, she came to and became aware of his presence. She tried to turn herself around towards him but remained stretched out on the sofa. "That you, Jon?"

"What happened?"

"Get us a drink, will yer?" He went into the kitchen and returned with a glass of water. He watched her struggle to lift the glass to her lips, then wince with pain as she drank. Even with an empty glass in her hand, her arm shook.

"Well, take the bloody thing!"

He took the glass back to the kitchen and returned to the living room. His mother had fallen back and was lying still again. He was not used to seeing her like this. All her angry energy seemed to have drained away from her so he watched her in a way that had never been possible before. She looked more feminine, more like the girls at school, younger, like the mother of the little girl in the park.

Jon moved about warily, in case his mother might rouse herself again, unsure whether to wake her or not. The sound of her breathing reached him, slow and even. Upstairs the house was a mess. The top panel of his door lay in splinters on the landing floor and all the drawers and cupboards in his room were open. In his mother's room, the bed lay tipped onto its side. A blood-stained towel confronted him just inside the door. He went back into his own room and closed the window.

Downstairs, he continued to watch his mother on the sofa. The wound was a broad strip of bruised flesh which reached from the side of her left eye down to the tip of her chin, and it disturbed him. Towards the top, near the eye, it was a livid, red colour. Around and below the mouth he could see the part of her face that had received the main force of the blow. The bruise was dark and threatening. He peered cautiously at her right eye, leaning over her. He noticed that this other eyelid was badly grazed and half closed.

Her breathing had become very shallow and he found himself listening anxiously for its reassuring rise and fall. What was going to happen? How much battering could she take? Would he have to take her to hospital? Should he call an ambulance? Unable to answer his own questions, he switched on the television. A few minutes later his mother stirred again.

"'Ow long you bin like this?"

"Since that bastard went this morning."

"What 'appened?"

"What d'yer bleedin' think?"

"You all right, then?" Her head fell back. She was exhausted again. "D'yer want me to do anything?"

"Yeah, get us a cup a tea." Reassured, Jon retreated to the kitchen. His mother dozed.

When he returned, he looked around at the mess and put the tray down on the table. "Here y'are then." He watched her and she stirred – he would not have to touch her. He passed her the cup and she drank quickly. "What did 'e do this for?"

"'E found you'd got yer bike back – Christ, was 'e mad about his car. Thought he was going to come on real 'eavy with you, like." She took another mouthful of tea and they were silent for a moment. She lay there, quiet and very still – she needed the time to recover her thoughts after the violence that still dominated the room. She looked back on all the shouting and raised fists across the years – fighting, always bleedin' fightin'. The memories raised themselves in her mind like old black and white photographs, sharp yet distant. She could just hold on to the images but she had neither the stamina nor the will to think about them.

The boy watched his mother, absorbed in her injuries and her exhaustion. He remembered Old Fisher finding him after the encounter with Bill in school. Words and anger between him and this woman had been one thing – but this was new violence, brought in from outside. He wanted none of it in their home, or whatever you called the bloody place.

Later, she came to again. "I weren't going to have the bleedin' house knocked about. Soon as I told him, he got a bit mad with me, like."

"You aren't gonna see 'im again?"

"What do you think?"

Now she could see her dad, outside the apartment where she had waited while he went to sort out Chris. She paused and made another effort to think. She had not had a man – and perhaps the chance of something more permanent – for some time. Despite the hope, despite the prospect of sorting out this son, the chance of a different life, something deep inside had warned her against the man, but she had not found the energy, the determination to take any notice.

"I just ain't got the strength for this bleedin' carry-on." Jon felt the weariness of her thirty-two years.

"You goin' down the hospital?"

"Nah – too many questions. You'll 'ave ter ring in sick for me tomorrer."

"We got anything to eat?"

"Bit a' bread and jam, I think."

Jon thought of the chippy. He recalled the smell of fish and chips and remembered the money in his pocket.

"I'll just pop down the chippy. You okay?"

There was no answer for a moment. His mother had finished her tea and had started to doze off again.

"You okay?"

For a moment she roused herself. "Yeah."

There were no kids at the chippy. A man in white overalls watched Jon as he entered. Jon ignored him and looked up at the menu.

"You decidin' what to nick off the little kids?"

"Two cod and chips, mate."

"Yer tryin' ter con me now, are yer?"

Jon was angry but he was also hungry. "There's yer bleedin' money." He handed over a fiver and the man held it up to the light to scrutinize it.

"Bloody 'ell, it's genuine – you must 'a' nicked it."

But he turned away and started to serve up the fish and the chips. The smell tortured Jon who stood and watched the familiar ritual, wondering just how hungry his mother was.

There was no thought of what she might like to eat, or what might be good for her to eat as she tried to recover. Jon had put together a lack of food in the house, his own hunger and the possibility that his mother might be hungry. He could not imagine anything else – had the little girl in the park been hungry rather than frightened, fish and chips is what he would have got her.

"There y'are." The man looked him straight in the face this time. "See yer."

His mother was pleased with her supper. She roused herself when she smelt the chips and almost snatched them from him. Cautiously, she swung her legs round off the sofa. Jon saw the bruises on her thighs. She clutched the parcel of food on her lap and ate with surprising speed.

"That was all right. D'yer think you could make a cuppa?"

He brought her a mug and turned to go back to the kitchen where he was going to drink his own tea.

"'Ere, 'ow d'yer manage to pay for them chips? You ain't bin nickin' again, 'ave yer?"

"Nah."

"Must 'ave cost at least a fiver. Where d'yer get the money?"

"Did a job for someone."

"Who?"

"Dunno 'is name." Jon went to get his tea. When he returned his mother seemed more composed.

"Ah don't want anyone else coming round 'ere complainin' like – yer know, like Old Ma Butty." Jon realised that nothing more had happened about his visit to Old Butty's house. He had not given the matter a moment's thought for days. They drank their tea.

"Is 'e gonna come back again?"

"Dunno. There's no telling with bastards like 'im."

"What'll yer do if 'e comes back?"

"Tell 'im ter piss off – 'e's not smashin' this bleedin' place up again."

Jon felt relieved. "What did yer let 'im take me bike for?"

Before, he would have expected an angry reply, but she was getting tired again. "I was getting sick a' you nickin' from me, that's why. Nothin' was safe with you about, Jon." She looked straight at him. "You won't let 'im in if 'e comes back, will yer?"

"Nah."

He felt trapped by the question – there was no other answer that he could give; there was no hurry to produce an answer but he could think of nothing else to say. He took the mugs back to the kitchen and rinsed them under a tap. When he returned, his mother was asleep.

He went upstairs, collected pieces of smashed furniture and took them out to the bins at the back of the house. He pulled back his mother's curtains and let in the last of the evening light. There was enough to show the damage that the fighting had caused. One drawer had come clean out of the chest. He picked it up, filled it with some of the mess on the floor and returned it to its place. The wardrobe door had reached the opposite side of the room. He slid it out onto the landing and dumped it there, then returned to tip the bed back flat on the floor. Three of the flimsy legs had been smashed off. Jon managed to unscrew the remaining one so the bed was level. He left the bedclothes where they where, a tangled knot, piled up in a corner of the room.

Apart from the door, Jon's room had sustained little damage. The bed and its crumpled sheets had not been touched. Only the drawers in the little cabinet had been turned out and the shelves in the wardrobe swept clear. In a few moments he had restored the room to something better than its usual state.

Downstairs his mother levered herself upright, knocking over a chair as she did so. The sound reached Jon – he hurried down to her and they came face to face in the hallway.

"I'm going upstairs. Give us a hand."

She struggled onto the first stair and he stood awkwardly behind her, trying to take her elbow. She paused after a few steps and he sensed her misery; it matched her straggling hair and the stains on her wrap. She moved on and, eventually, they reached the top.

"You'd better get some kip."

She nodded her head then hobbled across the landing and into her room. Then she called to him: "Come and give us a hand, Jon." He went. "Can't see a thing in here – can you find a spare bulb somewhere?"

By now it was dark. He went back into another room to find a replacement for the solitary bulb. He returned and stayed there long enough to tidy her bedclothes, under her direction. He felt uncomfortable with her in her own room and wanted to get away. Soon she settled, crouching down on the low bed, and Jon returned to his own room.

He slept well and was up by seven the next morning. For the first time in years he went into his mother's room and called to her: "All right, Mum?"

"Dunno yet." She roused herself. "You gonna make some tea? Can you make us some toast?"

He returned with a mug in one hand and a plate in the other. "There y'are. Feeling a bit better, are yer?"

His mother picked up her toast for a moment, put down the plate and took a mouthful of tea. "A lot bleedin' better than yesterday." She continued with her breakfast. "You'll have to help me get sorted later." She looked at him closely. "You going into school?"

"Suppose so."

"Fer Christ's sake don't get me into any more bother over that." He said nothing. "You'll have to get a few things when you come back, okay?"

"Yeah. I'll see to it."

It was only quarter to eight when he picked up his jacket.

"You're going out early."

"Yeah – I gotta see someone." He turned and was gone.

Jon met Paul just as he was unlocking the garage doors. On his way to work he had thought of little else. He had thought of the money he would add to the little wad in his pocket, and he thought again of keeping it safe somewhere. He thought about the customer's approval of him the day before and still felt the glow of Paul's obvious satisfaction.

It was a good start to a working day. Jon recalled school and his other problems but they didn't bother him somehow. He enjoyed this.

Later, Paul showed him how to clean an engine that had been removed from a car. It was coated with thick, black grease and oil. Even as the two of them moved it around, they found themselves covered in muck. Jon had yet to get used to working with filthy hands and did not like the loss of control once they were really greasy. Neither did he like walking through the streets covered in oil – it gave away too much.

"Bloody 'ell – look at that bleedin' shit! It'll be all over me shirt."

For a moment they stopped trying to lift the engine. Paul straightened his back. "Right. Just 'ang about a moment." He turned to a cupboard, wrenched open the door and pulled out a grimy and tatty-looking boiler suit. "'Ere y'are. Put this on for now. I'll get yer a new one on Monday."

Jon started to pull himself into the overall. Paul steadied the engine and watched Jon struggle with the unfamiliar outfit. "Come on – we ain't got all day!"

"Well I'm buggered if I'm gonna get any more grease on my things." Jon finished changing and rolled up the sleeves, which were rather long. They got the engine into position and Paul took up a brush and a pot of engine cleaner, a foul-smelling mixture of oil and diesel. "'Ere y'are. Just wet it all over like this, so it soaks in first, then brush it hard to get the muck off." Jon watched as the action of the brush sprayed the filthy black liquid all over the place.

"Christ, what a bleedin' job."

Paul laughed then noticed Jon's expression. "No one said this was a clean job. You're not working in an office, yer know." He laughed again. "You wouldn't like being in an office anyway – too much like that bloody school of yours!" Jon half-smiled at the thought. "Anyway, this is important – you try working on an engine that's covered with all this shit!"

Jon accepted the explanation and continued with his efforts. Soon, however, the smell and the constant splashing annoyed him. He watched as Paul removed some new parts from their boxes and set them out on a bench. The man looked up and Jon returned to his task. Jon was leaning over to reach to the back of the engine when he knocked over the large pot containing the cleaning mixture.

"Oh fuckin' shit!" Jon flung down the stiff brush he had been using.

"Now what 'ave yer done?"

"It's gone all over me bloody foot."

"You'll learn soon, you will." Paul was grinning, trying not to laugh.

"Don't see what's so bloody amusing." Jon kicked the pot which rattled its way across the workshop, then turned and slipped on the brush. Paul roared with laughter and leant against the workbench.

"Stick yer fuckin' job!" Paul continued to laugh and the boy stormed out into the sunshine. He walked around to the waste bins and leant against the wall. He was not there long before he kicked out savagely at one of the bins and marched across to the café.

Jimmy was clearing the tables. "What you want to bring that stink in here for?" He saw the expression on Jon's face. "Oh. What's up with you then?"

"Where's me fuckin' bike?"

"I thought you wanted me to keep it safe."

"I ain't 'aving anyone laughing at me like that. Look at me bloody things." Jimmy grinned – Jon was still wearing the old boiler suit that Paul had given him.

"Tried lookin' at yerself in the mirror? You can't go 'ome like that. Your mum wouldn't know yer." Jimmy knew that Jon was serious but there was no chance of keeping a straight face.

"I'm off. I ain't puttin' up with this shit!"

"You stop outside with that 'orrible smell. I'll lose all me customers if you stay in 'ere." Jon did not move. Jimmy went through to the back of the kitchen and returned with Jon's bike. Jon followed him outside. There was no sign of Paul.

"You'd better get out of them things – you can't go home like that." Jon caught sight of himself in the café window and started to wriggle out of the oily suit. As he struggled, he moved uncomfortably from one wet foot to the other.

"You got yer money?"

Jon stopped.

Jimmy continued. "You want yer money, don't yer?"

"Oh fuck!"

"Never mind, 'Oh fuck!' You didn't think of that when you lost your temper." Jon looked straight at him but said nothing. "Get out of that boiler suit for a minute. That's right, just leave it down there. Come out the back and get yerself tidied up a bit. I've got some

149

clean things out there." Jimmy wheeled the bike back through the kitchen and Jon followed him.

Paul grinned at Jon when he shuffled back into the garage. "Oh, you're back again." Beyond Paul, Jon could see the engine which was now clean. Paul held a large wad of grimy cloth in one hand and held both arms out in an open gesture. "Welcome back. I'll have to show you how to clean engines some time." Jon couldn't smile but he stood there and listened. "Come on. Let's get the engine back over here, then we'll have a cuppa."

When Jon returned home just after six o'clock his mother was waiting for him. "You're late. Where'yer bin?"

"Did a job for someone on the way home." He felt his back pocket.

"You'll 'ave to hurry up before the shop shuts – we need a few things." She went to a drawer in the kitchen.

"Shit! You got any money, Jon?"

"'Ow much? Fiver enough?"

"Should be. This is what we want." She handed him a list.

"When'll yer pay me back?" He asked the question reluctantly; part of him just wanted to pay, to do his bit without bothering his mum, but he feared her ready suspicion. She must not realise that he had a steady source of money.

"End a' the week – when I get me allowance." She gave him a scrap of paper and he set off.

Jon had just paid for the pies in the corner shop when he became aware of Dean standing next to him. Dean watched as the shopkeeper handed Jon change, then spoke to one of the assistants. "Two packets of King's."

The assistant turned to look along the shelves of cigarettes. Dean turned to Jon. "No money again. What this then?" Dean snatched at the fiver in Jon's hand.

"Piss off – it's me old lady's."

Dean continued to look straight at him, and sneered. "Yeah?"

"I'm on an errand."

"That's two pound forty-eight." Dean pulled out a fiver and handed it over. "You fuckin' expect me to believe that? Yer old woman's money and you doin' a bleedin' errand as well?"

"She ain't well."

"Here's yer change." Dean slid the coins into his pocket.

Jon swept up his paper bag and moved towards the door. Dean turned to follow. He called out, "'Ere, 'ang about!", but Jon had gone.

Outside Dean could see Jon, fifty yards away, walking towards his home. Jon glanced back over his shoulder and saw Dean struggling to trot after him. Jon walked on quickly and deliberately so that Dean was puffing when he finally managed to catch up.

"Hold up, yer goin' too bleedin' fast."

Jon grinned a little savagely, but he did not slow up. He enjoyed the advantage and pressed on. "What's up then?"

"Our Billy's still bloody mad about that money – you know – what you owe 'im, like."

"I tell yer, I ain't got no money – and me cousin's taken 'is bike back. I'm nigh-on skint."

Jon celebrated this victory. He pressed on with longer strides. He lifted his head and looked ahead along the road. In his mind's eye he could see Dean, desperate to keep up to ask his babyish questions, to plead in his petty thief's way for his big brother's money.

At the corner he was a few yards ahead. He turned to let Dean think that he might catch up.

"See yer, Dean." He walked on. A moment or two later he realised that he was alone.

Back indoors, he sat with his mother while they ate their pies in front of the television. Soon, the programme was interrupted by advertisements and Jon picked up the rubbish and went out. In the kitchen he easily found some space when he came to put the things down, and realised that something had changed. Normally, food, dirty mugs and the few clean items that he could ever find struggled for space. Often they nudged one another over the edge – and Jon's bare feet would find the small sharp pieces of broken crockery that were the result of these frequent fatalities.

Now there was space. There were no dirty things and several clean items were stacked, out of the way, on the corner of the worktop.

There was a knock at the door, a heavy knock. It was twice repeated, an insistent knock, a knock that demanded attention.

"See who it is will yer, Jon?"

The persistence irritated Jon who was beginning to enjoy his evening at home. His mother would not trouble him and there was food and the television. This was a strange but pleasant sensation for him and he did not want it disturbed. It was something to protect so that he could think more about it. Again, someone hammered on the front door.

"You going, Jon?"

Reluctantly, he got to his feet. A voice called through the letter box, something about opening the fucking door. Jon paused. It was the last voice that he wanted to hear and it was interrupting his peace of mind, this new state of being. He walked out through the hall and opened the front door. "What do you want?"

"Fuckin' criminal damage to my car, that's all."

"Criminal damage to our fuckin' house."

For a few seconds, they glared at one another. Jon realised that he was keeping a tight grip on the door.

"Yer mum in?"

"She don't want ter see yer."

"I don't want your bleedin' lip."

"She don't want ter see yer."

The man stepped onto the threshold. Jon did not budge, so they were face to face.

"You there, Tina?"

There was no reply.

"I know yer there. I wanna see yer."

Still there was no reply.

"You've no bleedin' right to fuck me about like this. What d'yer think yer playin' at?" Being ignored so pointedly did not suit Dave. "You ain't gonna treat me like this, you stupid bloody cow!" He turned to Jon who had not moved a muscle. "And as fer you, yer little shite, you'll be seeing me again!"

Dave did not expect the shove. As the door slammed, his sleeve caught in the jamb. He pulled it free, kicked the door and added to what he had already said. Out on the path he was silent, as if he had run out of words. From the living room, Jon's mother watched him drive away.

Chapter Fifteen

It was still warm in October. Even in the middle of the month the summer's sense of ease and well-being remained. It was a fine autumn.

Jon looked fit and well. Over the last four months he had put on weight and had lost the pasty, pale look that had hung over him. He pushed the bike into the outhouse in the back yard and locked the door. He used the bike for work every day now. Somewhere, hidden away, a post office book bore witness to what he had earned over the summer. At night he slept more soundly.

"Thought you said you was goin' into school." His mother had returned home from her job just before him. She turned and picked up a sheet of paper from the table.

"What d'yer mean?"

"You lying little sod. This come today."

It was a letter from the school. Had Jon enrolled at another school? Was he ill? Was there any other reason for his failure to attend school? Unless there was an immediate and satisfactory reply the matter would be placed in the hands of the local authority's attendance officer. It was likely that legal proceedings would follow, especially in the light of Jon's appalling attendance record during the previous term.

"You stupid little sod. What d'yer want to go and do this to me for?" He knew that her plea was real and he watched her helplessly as she ground out a cigarette in a saucer and lit another one. "You are so bloody stupid. You were going to go in to school most days to keep 'em 'appy like while you kept yer little job. What are we goin' ter do now?"

Jon was thinking. For a moment, the self-assurance of the good summer months wavered. "I dunno. Just let me think for a bit." He reached out for his mother's packet of cigarettes and took one.

"Gotta string 'em along till Christmas – they won't bother after then."

"What d'yer mean?"

"I keep tellin' yer – they won't bother when I get near to leaving time – next Easter."

"So, what yer gonna do till then – get me fined? You gonna pay the fines?"

"Don't keep goin' on about it." He was pacing up and down now. "Let me think for a minute." His mother looked up at him from across the table.

"Well, you're a clever one. You're gonna drop me right in it now, ain't yer?"

Next morning he felt obliged to put in some time in at school, if only to stop his mother from worrying so much. On the way, he stopped at a phone box, rang Paul and told him he would be late. As he turned out of the phone box, he met the tall girl, Tracey. She was alone.

"Whatcha, Jon." She looked him up and down. "Long time, no see. Where y'bin?"

"'Ere 'n' there."

"You ain't coming in ter school, are yer?" He said nothing, but continued in the same direction, walking alongside her. He had grown taller during the summer and she no longer towered over him.

"They think you've moved, or gone to another school. Yer know what they're like, always asking bleedin' questions."

"You still got Old Lambert this year?"

"Yeah, silly cow." Tracey smiled. "She still fancies yer – always askin' about yer." Jon smiled too. The girl continued. "Reckon they get paid fer keepin' us in school?"

"Dunno."

They walked on slowly, saying nothing. From time to time, Jon looked around at her. She looked the same to him, yet he was no longer bothered by her. The urge to escape her had evaporated. They passed the old car and stopped by the corner shop where he had run errands for his mother.

"'Ang about, I'll just get some fags."

"Hiya, Jon. You okay?" He was better known in the shop now.
"Yeah. Twenty Marlboro."

The woman reached the packet from the shelf. "There y'are. 'Ow's things, then?"

"Okay." She handed him his change. "Ta. See yer."

"See yer, then."

Outside, he handed the girl a cigarette and they stood and smoked on the street corner. A few younger children went past on their way to junior school.

"What yer gonna tell Old Lambert? You've bin off fer over a bleedin' fortnight already and Old Fisher'll do 'is pieces too when 'e sees yer."

"Dunno yet. Yer know what it's like. Get in the fifth year and they don't bother yer after a while." They walked on in silence, swinging slowly along with their hands in their pockets. They stared at the pavement in front of them; an invisible hand seemed to choreograph their movements so that they kept pace with each other.

"What yer doing with yerself – yer got money for fags and that."

"Oh, this and that. Try and get a job some time."

"Buggered if I want a job. Go on the social, like our Laura." Jon thought of a shorter, thick-set version of his companion. "Anyway, I can leave early like, at Easter."

After registration Jon was not surprised to find himself in Mr. Fisher's office.

"Oh, you're back now – summer holiday finished, is it?" Jon said nothing. He was still sitting on one of the chairs outside the deputy headmaster's room. He didn't bother to look up. "I suppose you'd better come in.

Jon followed into the office and sat down without waiting to be asked. "That's it – make yourself comfortable." The teacher sat down opposite Jon and tried to continue. "Nearly five weeks of term and we've hardly seen you, Jon. That's why we had to write to Mum. Where have you been? You can't leave school until Easter. You know that, don't you?"

"Yeah."

"So why haven't you been in school?" The man sat back in his chair and looked across at Jon. "You know what'll happen if you're not in school, don't you?"

Jon remained silent. He had not yet learnt to hide a smile and one chose this moment to emerge. Apart from anything else, it relieved the boredom. Jon knew that really he was just a nuisance, an irritating one.

"I don't know what you're smiling for – you're in serious trouble. I've got to give the attendance officer some reason for your absence." For a second, Jon almost felt sorry for Mr. Fisher – he was obviously a lot older than Paul and a lot more care-worn. Jon remembered a time when he would have laughed at the man but he had a life to defend now.

"Gonna look at another school."

Mr. Fisher looked up and started to speak but Jon continued.

"Ah've bin unhappy here – ain't really bin gettin' on, 'ave I?" Mr. Fisher found himself nodding for a moment, then ignored the boy's cheek to see what he would say next.

"Well I ain't, 'ave I? Can't settle – don't get on with me teachers. Might as well go to another school. I'm miserable here." Jon paused for a moment, wondering whether to continue. "Me mum says I'll be better off making a fresh start somewhere else." He watched the teacher, waiting to see what he would have to say. "We're gonna try Park School."

"Do you know if they've got any places? You can't just go from one school to another – you'll have to make an official application." The man looked at him with suspicion. "You've discussed this with your mother?" Jon nodded. "Why isn't she here this morning? It's all very well you coming to me like this, but it's her I should be speaking to." There was another pause and then the phone rang. A conversation continued for several minutes and then Mr. Fisher turned again to Jon. "Can I get her at work?"

"I dunno – she ain't been too well of late." This was always a safe claim with his mother.

"Can I get her at home?"

"Well, er, we're 'avin' bother with the phone at the moment."

"She really ought to come up to school to see me if she's thinking of moving you. I'll have to write to her. I could probably come round if she's stuck at home, or ask the attendance officer to come." He watched to see how this went down with Jon.

"Yeah, I'll tell her." The teacher started to make a few notes. "That it now, Sir?"

The teacher jerked up his head to look at Jon who was already on his feet. There was a knock at the door. Another student stood there. "Yes. I'll have to see you later. Come and see me tomorrow."

Jon walked back home, collected his bike and set off to work. Paul was already busy.

"All right? Sorted?"

"Yeah. No bother." Paul and Jimmy rarely mentioned school.

He pushed his bike to its usual place, hung up the light jacket he was wearing and climbed into a new boiler suit.

"Can yer get that Volkswagen over the pit – I've nearly finished here." Jon fetched the keys; another day had begun.

On his way home that night, Jon met Barry, Steve's friend. Jon was walking – he was on his way to the shops in the town centre and had left his bike at work.

"'Ow's it goin', young Jon?"

"Okay. Bit a' bother with school, but that's sorted."

"What d'yer mean?"

"Told the stupid bastards I'm not 'appy at school – gonna get a transfer. That'll keep them off me back for a while longer."

Barry laughed. "Yeah, you've got the idea." He lit a fag. "Seen Old Steve lately? 'E was askin' for yer in the pub the other night."

"I'll look in tonight – I ain't 'ad a pint fer weeks."

They parted and Jon went on to the shops. His mother was pleased with the bits and pieces he brought home and she asked little about his jobs. Until this morning she had not troubled him about school for some time. And they had seen no more of Dave.

Around the next corner Jon ran into him. He was outside a shop. As he looked up at Jon a woman detached herself from his side and went into the shop. Jon noticed a boy with him who said something quickly to his father then followed after his mother. The man took Jon by the arm and propelled him across to the other side of the road.

"My kid's just told me – you're the thievin' bastard what stole money from 'im last term. And there's that fuckin' damage yer did to me car." Jon said nothing, but just eased the man's grip on his arm. "Your mother's such a stupid cow – no wonder you're such a thievin' bastard. You're shit – you're goin' nowhere."

Jon could see the kid over by the shop doorway. Dave followed his gaze, then turned back to Jon. "Don't you go near my kid again." The grip on his arm was tightened and Jon tensed himself for the blow. "You do an' I'll fuckin' kill yer. D'yer hear?"

Jon thought of the woman who had gone into the shop. "Yeah, an' I'll tell yer old woman about you screwin' my mum and knockin' 'er about. She'll be right chuffed."

Jon retrieved his arm and was gone.

If you have enjoyed this book

and would like to find out about Peter Inson's next novels,
or would like to order further copies of this one,

Go to: www.peterinson.net

On the Side

Despite the attempts of his uncle and his mother to stop him,
Alex discovers who his father is. But he has to find him.
As he approaches his father, Alex meets other members
of the family and has to deal with them too.

The Redundant Car Park

A novel in progress, set in 2025 in one of the home counties,
where the cloning industry is established underground and
there is a market for its products.

Further copies of **dunno** can be obtained by writing to
Charles Kimpton Publishers, 15 Priory Crescent, Wembley,
Middlesex HA0 2QQ and enclosing £6 plus £1.50
towards postage and packing.

dunno is also available through bookshops.